ERNESTINE

A Novel

by

E.B. SANCHEZ

Glassmill Press

ebsanchez.com

Copyright © 2015 E.B. Sanchez

ISBN-10: 0-9970266-0-X
ISBN-13: 978-0-9970266-0-3

ebsanchez.com

Published by Glassmill Press

To the Three Most Important Men in My Life:
Raul, Marc, and David

My life would not be what it is without you.
Thank you!

Table of Contents

Chapter 1
Jonathan

Sleep. Wonderfully-soothing sleep. It stops the pain and Ernestine was in pain. Not physical pain but emotional pain. In her sleep, happiness swirled around her like snowflakes on a brilliant Christmas Eve.

Jonathan was holding her, caressing her, whispering in her ear. She stretched luxuriously in the big, soft bed and wished that it would always be like this. But then a door slammed and Ernestine woke up. It took her a few seconds to realize that it had been but a dream. Jonathan was not here, he would never be here again. Ernestine felt tears stinging in her eyes.

She closed her eyes and his image lingered around the edges of her mind. She remembered the first time she laid eyes on Jonathan so many years ago at that lawyers' conference in Chicago. She remembered the blistery autumn morning, mist rising from the lake and a fierce wind howling down North Michigan Avenue, where the Hotel Intercontinental was located.

Ernestine attended the conference together with her father, a prominent Boston lawyer. Jonathan was one of the key speakers and an acquaintance of her father's. Ernestine had not really wanted to go to this event as they were usually boring; and listening to speakers who are only interested in hearing themselves talk was not one of Ernestine's favorite pastimes.

But when it was Jonathan's turn to speak, she was riveted to his person. His eloquence, his elegance, and charm ensnared her; and before she knew it, he was standing beside her, deep in conversation with her dad.

After what seemed to her an eternity, both men turned and her father introduced her to Jonathan, his new junior partner in his law offices in San Diego. After the prescribed formalities, Jonathan asked her:

"Ernestine, would you do me the honor of dining with me tonight?"

"Oh yes," Ernestine stammered and felt like an utter fool.

"I'll pick you up at 7pm in the lobby, okay?"

For Ernestine, the rest of the afternoon dragged on and the speeches seemed never-ending. Finally, her father rose and led her to the elevator.

"Have a good time tonight my dear. Jonathan is a very special person." With these enigmatic words, her father left her and went in search of his wife.

In her room, Ernestine dressed in her favorite green tailored suit that beautifully offset her long red hair and made her jade-green eyes shine. The only jewels she was wearing were a pearl necklace given to her by her grandmother and a narrow gold band on her little finger given to her by her childhood friend Robin. She carefully put on her make-up and chose a subtle lipstick that enhanced her perfectly-shaped mouth. A last satisfied look in the mirror and off she went to meet this handsome lawyer.

Jonathan was waiting for her in the lobby. He wore a dark suit and his long wavy blond hair was freshly washed. His shoes were shining and his fingernails were clean. He slowly advanced toward Ernestine.

"Hi, Ernestine; you look stunning. Your dad never told me he had a daughter as beautiful as you."

"Hi, Jonathan. Well my dad never told me about his handsome junior partner either."

Seeing the amusement in his eyes, she laughed and they left the hotel. An old moss-green cab that seemed to have been waiting for them at the curb took them to a little restaurant off the beaten path. The entrance was framed with an array of flower pots of all shapes and sizes. A few steps led to a cracked antique door and once inside, the smell of Italian cooking made her mouth water.

She ordered lasagna and a small green salad. Jonathan went for papardelle with a creamy tomato sauce, the specialty of the house. A bottle of Chianti was brought and the glistening red wine poured into tall stemmed glasses. Ernestine took a forkful of her lasagna and was amazed at the texture and delicate taste of it.

"This is delicious," she exclaimed, "However did you find this place?"

"Actually, years ago my parents brought me here. It was an old and shabby place at the time, but the food was as delicious then as it is today. It has been in the Morcote family since it opened its doors during Al Capone's reign."

"Al Capone? Was he a regular here?"

"Oh Ernestine, I would not know. I was not around at that time."

She laughed and told him that she had always had a fascination for the old crime families. They talked about crime and the legal system while savoring their food until Jonathan exclaimed:

"Enough! We hear about this all day long. Let's finish our meal and then go to a nightclub, if you are not too tired."

"Okay, let's go; and Jonathan, thank you for a delicious dinner."

They left the old restaurant and took a cab to a private club where Jonathan was a member. They had a couple of drinks, danced for a while, and then finally went back to the hotel. Jonathan accompanied her to her room and, before saying good night, he asked her:

"When are you coming to San Diego?"

"Next time my father flies out there I'll come with him," Ernestine promised; and looked at him with her big trusting green eyes.

The next day at breakfast, her father asked her about her evening and Ernestine blushed. "Oh ho," her father smiled, "you are quite taken with Jonathan; but understand, my Darling, he is quite a few years older than you are, and on top of that you are the boss's daughter. Quite a catch for the likes of Jonathan."

"Don't you like him? You were so full of praise before I went out with him last night."

"Of course I like him, I even respect him. But you are my little girl and I just want you to be happy and cared for."

"Daddy, it was just a dinner date; nothing happened. We just had a good time together. I promised him I'd come with you when you visit San Diego next time."

"Good. Your mother and I are going on Thursday. We'd like to look for a place to live; and if we like it, we're moving to the west coast. It's getting too cold here. So come with us and we'll make it a family outing. I'll tell my secretary to book us flights, a hotel, and a rental car. By the way, what are you up to today?"

"I'll have some shopping to do and I'll meet you later at the hotel, okay?"

"That's fine, Ernestine. Enjoy the day."

Ernestine walked up and down Michigan Avenue looking into the artfully-decorated shop windows, entering a boutique here and there, and finally ending up at 900 North Michigan. This was her mother's favorite place to shop for Christmas gifts.

After a couple of hours, she left with several colorful gift bags. Back at the hotel she decided to watch a movie and take it easy until it was time to have dinner with her parents. She could not get the handsome Jonathan out of her mind and was looking forward to meeting him again soon.

The trip with her parents to San Diego proved to be a life-changing event for Ernestine. She met Jonathan again and they had wonderful days exploring San Diego together. Jonathan took her to Sea World, the famous Zoo located among the hills at Balboa Park, Old Town with its picturesque houses, and the Mission de Alcala. He told her about the history of these places and Ernestine was amazed at his knowledge and ease with which he answered her questions. In the evening they dined in exclusive restaurants and spent the night dancing away in some nightclub or other. Ernestine felt so happy. When the day came to leave, Jonathan made a bold proposition to her father:

"Let Ernestine stay here with me. I'll show her more of Southern California and she could look for a place for you and your wife, Marge."

Ernestine was dumbfounded and so was her dad. But he recovered quickly and, glancing at his daughter, he agreed. They found a little cottage in Normal Heights where Ernestine spent the next few months. She lived like in a dream. During the day, she went house-hunting; and in the evenings, Jonathan would come by. Sometimes they went out and sometimes they cooked and just sat on the porch and talked about life, politics and their dreams.

One night stood out in Ernestine's memory like a brilliant star. It was June 6, and she and Jonathan had gone out for dinner to a classy Italian restaurant across the bay. The food was delicious, the wine superb and the view exceptional. On their way across the Coronado Bridge, Jonathan asked:

"Would you like to see where I live? I have something of a view and we can watch the sailboats from the balcony."

This was the first time Jonathan had invited Ernestine to his place and she was thrilled. However, she would not let him see her excitement.

"Sure, that would be lovely. A fitting end to a splendid evening."

Jonathan drove to his condominium in one of the towers framing San Diego Bay.

"I live on the 22nd floor. I hope you do not have vertigo," he smiled.

"We'll find out soon enough, won't we?" countered Ernestine.

The elevator opened into a beautifully-decorated foyer with oversized furniture that was very inviting to sit and rest awhile. Ernestine was taken aback. She never associated something like this with Jonathan. She had always pictured him as living in some house somewhere along the beach, with old and used furniture, clothes lying around, and last night's dinner dishes still in the sink. This place was extraordinary. Not only was it neat, it was clean and roomy.

Jonathan led her to a small sitting area off the foyer and brought her favorite drink: a Martini with white grape juice.

"Come, let's watch the sunset from the balcony," and he guided her to the other side of the apartment where huge French doors opened to an even bigger balcony furnished with sofas covered in red chintz, and chairs in royal blue. The many colorful pillows were very inviting.

Ernestine sat down and absorbed the view. As far as she could see was the immense, blue Pacific. The sun's golden rays were playing with the waves and warming the air. Ernestine felt like she was in a dream. Her head was spinning and her thoughts could not keep still.

She had known for some time that she was in love with Jonathan but as he never made a pass at her she just assumed that he did all this because she was the daughter of his boss. But then, she felt her Martini glass being taken from her hand and two strong arms embracing her.

When she opened her eyes, Jonathan's face was only inches away from hers. His dark brown eyes shone warm and his perfect mouth formed the words: *I love you,*

Ernestine. He held her tight and kissed her very gently so as not to disturb anything. Ernestine felt her blood rush from head to toe and then back again. She swayed in his arms, and all she could do to prevent herself from falling was to hold on to this wonderful man.

"Do you really mean what you just said?" asked Ernestine incredulously.

"I love you, and I have loved you for a long while," Jonathan answered, "I just was not sure how you would feel about this."

"Oh Jonathan, I think I fell in love with you the very first time I laid eyes on you, way back in Chicago."

"Well then, my sparrow, would you like to live here with me?"

"You are not serious, are you?"

"Of course I am. I finally found the woman I've been searching for, for so many years. Do you really believe I'd let her go again?"

Ernestine wanted to say something but Jonathan closed her mouth with a kiss and ever so gently led her to the sofa. He sat beside her and held her close, all the while playing with her red hair and whispering sweet words to her. Ernestine felt like in a dream. "This is not happening," she thought. "I must have had too much to drink"; and she slowly opened her slate-green eyes.

But it was not a dream. Jonathan was beside her, unbuttoning her blouse and playing with her nipples. He gently squeezed them and a sensation, almost painful, raced through Ernestine's body and made her head spin. She tried to sit up, but Jonathan gently pushed her back onto the soft pillows.

"Don't fret, my sparrow, I won't do anything you don't want me to do, okay?"

"Okay," whispered Ernestine; "but I have to tell you just one thing. I have never been with a man before and I don't know what to do."

Jonathan looked at her in amazement. "You are the most beautiful creature I have ever kissed in my life and to be the one who makes you a woman is the rarest gift I ever received."

Jonathan slowly and expertly removed all her clothes without ever stopping his caresses. Ernestine felt her body tingle all over and a need arose in her that she was not quite sure how to satisfy. She followed Jonathan's lead, and when he entered her it was like a fiery rod singeing her flesh; but it was just a fleeting pain and then they both were lost to their emotions.

"I love you," whispered Ernestine, "and I never ever want to leave you." With these words, she fell asleep. Jonathan carried her to his king-sized bed and laid her down on the crème-colored satin sheets. He kept on looking at her and made up his mind to love and cherish this woman for the rest of his life. When Ernestine awoke an hour later, Jonathan was still sitting in the rattan chair looking at her.

"What are you thinking?" Ernestine asked, concerned. She could see the frown on his face and was alarmed.

Jonathan got up and walked over to her, took her by the hand and headed toward the bathroom.

"Let's have a shower."

"Okay with me."

The bathroom was tiled in terra cotta and the faucets were bronze-colored. The tub was round with several water jets, and the shower sported several large and small shower heads. Ernestine felt like a young girl in the rain. The water felt warm and luscious on her body and she felt right at home with this man whom she had known but a few months. Yet to her, it seemed as if she had known him all her life. When she stepped out of the shower, Jonathan wrapped her into a soft teal bath sheet and guided her back to the bed.

"Hungry?"

"Somewhat."

He went to the kitchen and a few minutes later came back with a tray full of goodies. There were black and green olives, slices of cheese, water crackers, grapes, nuts, chocolate, and two glasses of champagne.

"This is wonderful!" exclaimed Ernestine, and looked up at Jonathan. He stood in front of her and took her hand and pulled her off the bed.

"I have to say something to you that I have never thought I would ever say. Will you marry me, Ernestine?"

Ernestine just looked at him and it took her but a moment to realize that this gorgeous man was proposing to her, he wanted her to be always by his side, to share his life and dreams with him. No other woman had ever been offered this opportunity. Ernestine felt dizzy and clung to Jonathan.

Her green eyes sparkled with a light from within as she whispered, "Yes, Jonathan, I will marry you and love you with all my heart always."

Jonathan kissed her and they fell back onto the bed and made love again. Tired but happy, Ernestine gently pushed Jonathan away and innocently asked:

"What about food? By now I am really starving. All these emotions made me very hungry."

"You are right. Let's have some of these nibblies and some champagne to celebrate our new life together.

"A toast to you and me and to a hundred years of happiness. Cheers!"

"Cheers!"

Jonathan then carried the empty glasses and the tray back to the kitchen. Ernestine could hear him rinse the glasses and she thought about what had just happened. She tried to hold on but sleep overcame her; and when she awoke late next morning, the golden sun was already high in the sky and Jonathan was nowhere to be seen. Ernestine got up and walked out onto the balcony where Jonathan was sitting in a chair reading the paper with a cup of black coffee beside him.

"Good morning, my sleepyhead," smiled Jonathan, and took her in his arms. "How is my bride this morning?"

"I slept and slept without waking up, not even once. You got yourself a real deal here."

"I know, I know; but now that you are awake I have a surprise for you." With that, he quickly went to the kitchen and came back with a lovely bunch of flowers.

"Home-grown, in the pots on the balcony."

"They are beautiful and the smell reminds me of my childhood. Thank you, my love. Thank you very much."

After breakfast on the balcony, they decided to spend the day in Julian, a little, charming town about one hour east of San Diego in the Cuyamaca Mountains. They browsed through the antique stores filled with all kinds of treasures. They found a quaint little bookstore that sold out-of-print used books, and they stopped at the Julian Café to eat some of the town's famous freshly-made apple pie. They wandered hand in hand around the town until late afternoon when they decided to head back.

Sitting on the balcony, overlooking the bay, they felt at peace. Jonathan looked at Ernestine and said:

"Let's get the marriage license first thing Monday morning, and with a bit of luck we can get married in July. What do you think?"

"Sounds great. Just let me tell my parents. I'd like them to be here with us on this special day."

"Would you prefer a big wedding with many people?"

"Oh, no," replied Ernestine horrified, "my parents and maybe some old friends if they can make it. What about you?"

"As you know, my parents are long gone. But some friends from college live here and it would be fun to celebrate with them. Let's make a list."

So they spent the evening planning their wedding, guessing at who might be coming to their wedding, and where to have dinner on that memorable day. Ernestine talked to her parents and told them of their plans. Her dad was not in the least astonished. He said to her:

"I wondered why it took Jonathan so long. The first time I saw you look at him, I knew that he was lost even though he did not yet know. But then I had an advantage over him. I know my daughter and he didn't."

"Oh Daddy, you knew more than even I did," pouted Ernestine.

Chapter 2
A New Beginning

Monday morning they got their marriage license and the wedding was scheduled for four weeks later. Ernestine's parents flew in from Boston a week earlier to help with the preparations. Invitations were sent out to their friends, the church was booked, the flower arrangements chosen, and the restaurant agreed upon.

Ernestine and her mother found the perfect wedding gown, an ivory-colored taffeta ball gown with beaded side-drape bodice, a sweetheart neckline, and pick-up skirt. A pair of satin gauntlet gloves and a rhinestone crystal headpiece was all that was needed to transform Ernestine into a fairy-tale princess.

Her mother chose a leaf-colored sleeveless brocade top with beading and chiffon skirt that underscored her flawless complexion and her sensual mouth. Happy with their purchase, they drove to Seaport Village. There, among the little quaint shops with all their knick-knacks, they found a table at the Pier Café and decided to celebrate the day with a delicious clam chowder and a tuna sandwich.

They were chatting about the wedding and the way the house-hunting was going. Ernestine had found a beautiful home that she was eager to show her mother. It was an older home in the Tudor style with an English cottage garden out front. Ernestine was sure that her mother, who had grown up in England and come to America as a child, would like it very much.

It was located at a corner on a quiet street in Coronado, not far from the beach, with a large backyard filled with old trees giving shade during the summer's heat. Ernestine and her mother finished their lunch and headed toward the car and took the freeway to the Coronado Bridge. When

Ernestine drove up to the house, her mother had tears in her eyes.

"This looks so very much like the house I spent so many happy years in as a child in England."

"Do you want to see it?" asked Ernestine.

"Oh please, let's see it," replied her mother while fishing for a handkerchief in her cumbersome handbag.

"The agent should be here any minute," said Ernestine.

They looked around the neighborhood with its stately homes and old-world ambience. The agent arrived and, after greetings, opened the house for them. It was a gem; and Ernestine's mother called her husband to ask him to come and look. He came and the deal was made. Her parents were to move into the house later that year.

Ernestine left them at the house and drove back to the apartment. She found Jonathan sitting on the balcony looking out over the blue ocean. He got up and took her into his arms and slowly kissed her.

Ernestine told him all about her day and that she and her mother had found the perfect place to buy their dresses. Jonathan watched her and was happy that her parents had finally found a house they liked.

The next couple of weeks passed very quickly. All the arrangements for the wedding were done, the guests had made their reservations, and tomorrow was the big day. Ernestine could hardly sleep; but finally, she dozed off to her own dream world.

Then the big day arrived. Ernestine, helped by her mother and her best friend, slipped into the lacy underwear, and put her wedding gown on. Her hair was held together with the headpiece and fell in red waves around her shoulders. She looked fabulous. The ivory color highlighted her red hair and made her green eyes sparkle.

Then her dad came to take her to the ceremony; and from that moment on her memory became fuzzy. She recalled that there was a white limousine taking them somewhere and then she was walking down the aisle on her father's arm and was given to Jonathan who was waiting for her by the altar dressed in a dark gray tailcoat. The minister started to speak and then it was over and she was Jonathan's wife.

Exiting the church there were all their friends congratulating them. Pictures were taken and then they proceeded to the Hotel Del where the wedding reception took place. Tired but happy, Jonathan took Ernestine home and carried her over the threshold, put her down on the sofa, and brought her a glass of champagne.

"A toast to you and me and the happiest day of my life!"

They clinked their glasses, sipped the golden liquid, and fell into each other's arms. They made it to the bedroom where they undressed and hopped into bed for a memorable night. Bright sunshine woke them up. They had fallen asleep without consummating their marriage.

They laughed and began packing their bags for their honeymoon. The plane was leaving in the afternoon for Kona. They honeymooned on the Big Island of Hawaii at a beautiful, secluded resort, perfect for their first time together as husband and wife.

They rented a car and drove around the island. They visited the Volcanoes National Park that is home to the world's largest volcano, Mauna Loa, and the world's most active, Kilauea. They walked through tropical forests and looked at the immense craters and lava flows that have scarred the landscape over many centuries.

One day, they had lunch at Waimea, a ranch town up in the mountain, when Jonathan took Ernestine's hand and looking into her big trusting eyes and said:

"My darling, I have not given you a wedding band. I want you to have this instead. It was my grandmother's. My mother wore it until she died and she had always told me this story: When I was little and asked my mother why she'd wear this beautiful ring to clean the house she'd answer:

"You see, my little one, this is a promise my husband, your dad, made me many years ago. As long as you wear this ring, no harm will come to you. I will protect you and love you always."

"I give this to you with the same promise, I will protect you and love you always, even after death," said Jonathan.

Ernestine looked at the ring. It was a beautiful 18-carat gold eternity band glittering with natural blue sapphires and diamonds.

"Oh Jonathan, it is superb. I don't know what to say. I am so honored to wear it always; and by doing so I promise that I will love and cherish you forever."

They strolled around the meadow for a little while without talking, each deep in thoughts. It was as if all of nature had been witnessing this solemn promise of these two people to one another and both, Jonathan and Ernestine could feel that something profound had just happened to their relationship ... something which would forever be with them.

The rest of the day they spent at the beach of the hotel, laying in the warm sunshine and enjoying the solitude that sometimes envelopes two souls that belong to one another.

After a lovely dinner on the lawn of the restaurant, they had a drink at the moonlight bar and then went up to their suite. They stepped out onto the balcony and watched the myriad of stars twinkling in the night sky, holding on to each other as if they were a part of the nightly universe.

Back inside, they started to make love, but slowly without hurry; and when their passion consumed them it was like nothing they had experienced before. They were overwhelmed with love, trust and respect for one another. They fell asleep in each other's arms and woke up the next morning feeling whole ... whole as they had never felt before; and they realized that their union was the reason for it.

The days flew by and soon it was time to take the plane and head back to everyday life. Well not quite, as this was the beginning of their new life together.

Chapter 3
An Outing

Deep in her sleep, Ernestine heard the phone ringing and the insisting noise brought her out of her dream. She was dazed for a moment but then remembered that something had happened; and it hurt so very much, it was better to sleep and dream. She drifted back into her uneasy slumber.

Life with Jonathan was an endless sequence of beautiful, peaceful days and nights. One day, they put their bikes on his black Ram pick-up truck and drove out to the countryside to Lake Morena. This little gem is located in the mountains east of San Diego. On this early spring day, the stony little beach was still deserted and the small, wooden cabins not yet rented.

They unloaded their bikes, strapped the picnic basket on her blue bike, and off they went. The dusty smell of the grasses and flowers reminded her of her childhood. They stopped under a big leafy tree and had some cold chicken breasts, some homemade potato salad, slices of cucumbers, and mineral water to quench the thirst. They were talking about life when suddenly, Jonathan felt a raindrop.

"I don't believe this. For once we go bicycling and it has to rain!" he exclaimed. "Come on, Ernestine. We have to get back quickly. Otherwise we are going to be soaked!"

Ernestine could not help herself. She was laughing so much that tears ran down her cheeks.

"It does not matter, Darling, we'll be fine," she answered. But nonetheless, she collected the remains of their lunch and put it back into the basket, climbed on the bike, and followed Jonathan back to the truck. The wind had increased and dust was flying all over. It was hard to see the way and Ernestine bumped against a stone and fell.

She was not hurt. Only her knees and elbows were scraped and she felt rather silly, sitting in the middle of the path with her lunch strewn around her and her blue bike looking rather gray and bent out of shape.

The rain started slowly. Big drops fell to the ground and made the dust jump as if hit by a hot poker. Jonathan had pedaled back and found her sitting on the ground, enjoying the rain on her face. He got off his bike and helped her collect her things and get her back on the bike. However, the front wheel looked like a sausage and it was impossible to ride on it.

"Oh well, I guess we'll have to walk." Ernestine said. She took Jonathan's hand and the two of them walked back through the rain hand in hand. They arrived at the pick-up, loaded their bikes, took off most of their soaked clothes, and hopped into the car. Jonathan turned on the heating and some music and they sat there for a long while, quietly watching the rain giving so freely of its life-sustaining gift.

Gently, Jonathan took her into his arms and kissed her on her inviting lips. Her nipples hardened under his touch. "Jonathan, let's go home first, so that we don't get caught by some stranger."

"Okay, as you wish but it is your loss" Jonathan said, smiling. They drove home through the pouring rain and, once there, hopped into the hot tub, sipping a glass of white Merlot.

"Thanks for the exciting day. I am spent and my knees and elbows are stinging. I think I will have a good night's sleep." With these words, Ernestine gathered the towel around her and went for the bedroom. By the time Jonathan followed a few minutes later, she was already fast asleep.

He undressed and joined her, but no matter how close he was holding her, she would not wake up. So he let her sleep "this one day, my darling, because you fell from the bike and I know that scrapes do hurt terribly," he said to himself.

Chapter 4
A Visitor

Ernestine did not hear the doorbell ringing, nor did she hear the knocking on her door or the voices in the large corridor. She kept on dreaming uneasily.

Jonathan and she were on their white sailboat that he had named after her nickname "Suri." She could not remember when or why she had gotten it but her parents always called her by this name. She remembered being in the garden of her grandparents' home in Chester, England, smelling the lovely flowers and chasing colorful butterflies. Her parents were sitting on the veranda together with her grandparents deeply engulfed in conversation.

Then she saw him. A small boy not much older than herself, with dark brown hair and the most trusting deep gray eyes she had ever seen. A small cap covered his unruly strands of hair, his lips were full and rosy, and he wore proper khaki shorts, a white shirt and a red tie.

"Want to help me catch butterflies?" Ernestine called to him.

The little boy approached and introduced himself as Robin Whittaker, the grandson of her grandparents' neighbors who was spending the summer with them as his parents were away on a trip around the world.

"I do not think it is appropriate to catch butterflies," he said to Ernestine very seriously. "They are living things and do not want to be caught, killed and exhibited on a piece of cardboard."

Ernestine was stunned. She had never intended to kill these ephemeral beauties. She merely chased them so she could run after something.

"Let us go and explore the banks of the small creek behind our house and see if we find some tadpoles," said Robin. Ernestine agreed, and off they went in search of tadpoles. Robin was a delightful boy to be with and Ernestine spent the whole summer exploring the surroundings with him. As the years went by and they grew older, they stopped spending the summers at their grandparents and so they lost touch with one another.

There would always be a birthday card and a Christmas card from Robin, and Ernestine would reply with a letter detailing the adventures of her life. She had invited Robin to her wedding but he excused himself telling her that he was on an important assignment for his newspaper and that it was impossible to replace him due to all the paperwork.

Ernestine accepted this as over the years, she had been eagerly reading Robin's documentaries of faraway places. He had become one of the top journalists of a main newspaper in Great Britain, and Ernestine was proud of him. However, she did not know much about his private life but assumed that he was married and had children.

Then one day, she got a phone call from Robin. He told her that he was in San Diego on assignment and would love to see her. Ernestine was thrilled. She invited him to her place, and a few minutes later the doorbell rang. Ernestine opened the door and was taken aback. A tall, devilishly-handsome man was standing there. His dark curling hair was cut short and his massive shoulders filled the coat he wore. His eyes were filled with warmth, and his smile was as intimate as a kiss.

"Robin," cried Ernestine, and put her arms around him. "Come in! It is good to see you again after so many years."

"Hello Suri," said Robin and held her tight. "It is good to see you too."

Something in his voice alerted Ernestine and she loosened his grip on her. For a fleeting moment she thought she had seen something close to despair in his eyes, but dismissed the thought. She led him to the balcony and Robin took in the gorgeous view of the bay. Ernestine served them ice cold lemonade sprinkled with fresh mint, and they sat down on the big, soft chairs and talked about their past.

Sometime later, Jonathan joined them and Robin described his life and work for the newspaper. He had seen most of the world, its beauty and also its ugliness. He talked about the slums of Sao Paulo, the utter poverty in Sudan, the little girl in Egypt whose eyes were covered with flies, the beauty of an Arizona sunset, the turquoise color of the Caribbean in Tulum, the impressive art collections at the l'Ermitage in St. Petersburg, the famous buildings he had seen, and the unknown people he had talked with. Ernestine and Jonathan were immersed in a world they had only read about; but Robin was able to bring it to life for them.

"No wonder you are such a sought-after journalist," said Jonathan. "You have the uncanny ability to make people feel what you have experienced."

"Thanks for the compliment," answered Robin, "and for your hospitality. I have to go as I have to get up very early tomorrow morning to drive down to Ensenada and see la Bufadora."

"La Bufadora?" asked Ernestine.

"Have you not been there yet? You live so close by and I have heard that it is quite a spectacle to behold, the water spouting out from an underground cave. Anyhow, it is time to go. Thanks again."

Ernestine brought him to the door and kissed him on the cheek. Robin looked at her, turned abruptly, and left without another word.

Ernestine thoughtfully closed the door and went to the balcony to rejoin Jonathan.

"He is in love with you," he said, "and it was painful for him to be here."

"What do you mean? We have known each other for eons, but we were never more than friends."

"That might well be, but...."

"But what?"

"Never mind; but do not be surprised if he does not come back."

Ernestine looked at the silvery moon hanging like a big penny in the sky, illuminating the bay and making the water glisten like snow.

"You know," she said to Jonathan," I had a strange feeling when he came there was something that he wanted to say, something I should have made him tell me, but I was too much of a coward. I did not want to ask because I did not want to hear the answer. I did not want to deal with his problems. And somehow I knew that it involved me. Does that make me a bad friend?"

"No, it makes you a cautious one, one that respects another's privacy and does not pry into somebody's heart out of curiosity."

For some time, they sat on the balcony, each one of them deep in thought, until Jonathan got up, pulled Ernestine into his arms and kissed her lightly on her soft lips.

"Come," he said, "let's forget about this for tonight. I have some other ideas right now." The smile in his eyes contained a sensuous flame that Ernestine recognized immediately.

"You never tire of me, do you?"

"No."

He swept her off her feet and carried her to their bedroom where he gently lowered her on the huge king-sized bed. He slowly started to undress her, first her Italian sandals, then he leisurely unbuttoned her blue-and-white-striped blouse and let it slip to the floor, he slowly unzipped her jeans, and pulled them off. Slowly and seductively, his gaze slid over her lacy dark blue bra and the matching panties. A wave of pleasure washed over Ernestine and her body ached for his touch.

"Not so fast," he whispered into her ear while her heart was hammering furiously. He kissed the tip of her nose, careful not to touch her, then her eyes; and finally, he kissed her on her mouth, his lips sending shockwaves throughout her entire body. She felt like she was on a sailboat rocking gently to the surreal music of the waves. Her whole being was yearning for his touch.

When he finally freed her breasts from the bra and his tongue caressed her sensitive swollen nipples, a deep sigh escaped her. Her body arched and his hand traced a path down her ribs to her stomach. His soft hands ever so slowly explored every inch of her, stopping here and there, massaging the inside of her thighs, finding their way up her arms to her palms, and down to her silken belly where he finally pulled off her panties.

He accidentally touched her and a shiver ran up and down her body, her breath came in short intervals, and her need grew to explosive proportions. He eased himself onto her and gently entered her, pushing slowly, freeing her in a bursting of sensations.

Her thoughts fragmented while the turbulence of his passion swirled around her. Their bodies were in exquisite harmony with one another, contentment and peace flowing between them. Ernestine snuggled close to Jonathan and fell asleep almost immediately, while Jonathan was wide awake, marveling at the woman beside him. When the first light timidly illuminated the western sky, Jonathan finally fell into a deep, dreamless sleep.

Chapter 5
Reprieve

"Ernestine, Ernestine, open the door!"

Slowly, Ernestine opened her eyes, awakened by the voices in the hallway calling her name. It took her a while to realize where she was, and then it hit her like a thunderbolt: Jonathan! Jonathan was dead, killed in a car accident.

Slowly, the painful realization came back. The police had come to her door and told her that there had been an accident on Telegraph Canyon Road in Chula Vista. An unidentified driver going west had hit the median, plowed through a tree and landed on an oncoming car ... Jonathan's silver Porsche. Both drivers were killed instantly. So sorry; need to come and identify the body.

"Do you have someone we can call and that can come with you?" the policewoman asked gently. Ernestine was numb, but handed her a business card.

"You want me to call Kevin Masters?"

"Please."

Kevin, a partner at Jonathan's law firm and his long-time friend, arrived a few minutes after he received the call from the police. He made the arrangements and took Ernestine to the morgue. The badly-mangled body did not look like Jonathan's, but it was his face. Not a scratch was on his beloved face.

Ernestine fainted and was taken home. The law firm took care of the funeral arrangements, and all Ernestine remembered was the service. It was held at the Immaculate Conception on the grounds of the University of San Diego campus.

The church was decorated with beautiful flowers, candles were lit, and a solemn group of people was attending. His law partners were the pallbearers and a couple of close friends supported Ernestine. When she passed the coffin, she touched it lightly so as to say farewell. It was a very touching moment. Bishop Maher celebrated the mass, and afterwards Ernestine was taken home. Mary-Ann, Kevin's wife and a medical doctor, gave her a sedative and put her to bed.

"Sleep now; we'll be back in a few hours," she told Ernestine and gently closed the bedroom door.

"Ernestine!" yelled another voice. And this time, Ernestine got out of bed and walked hesitantly toward the door and opened it.

"Thank God, you are okay," said Mary-Ann. She took Ernestine into her arms and led her to the sofa.

"I brought you some food. You need to eat something."

"I am not hungry," whispered Ernestine. "Please just leave me alone."

"Sorry, but we cannot leave you by yourself," said Mary-Ann. "I will pack some things for you and then you and I are going to a spa where we will be pampered for a couple of weeks and after that we'll see what we do."

Ernestine knew that it was useless to argue with Mary-Ann, and she also knew that Mary-Ann and Kevin were right. God only knows what she would do if left alone. Still under sedation, Ernestine let Mary-Ann pack her things and then she left with them. Kevin took them to the airport and they boarded a plane.

Ernestine had no idea where they were going and she could not care less. All she knew was that Jonathan was forever gone from her life. He would never look at her again, never speak to her again, never kiss her again, and never make love to her again. The thought of facing a life without him was too much for Ernestine. She silently cried and nestled into her first-class seat. Mary-Ann took her hand and gave her a pill.

"Take this," she said. "It will make the pain go away."

Obediently, Ernestine swallowed the pill and dozed off. Mary-Ann was watching her; and when a smile touched Ernestine's face, she knew that she was dreaming of happier times.

Only too soon did the flight attendant announce that they were landing in San Juan. Mary-Ann and Kevin had chosen Puerto Rico for this stay as Ernestine had never been here with Jonathan.

Ernestine and Mary-Ann were met at the curb by the hotel bus. The driver loaded their luggage and helped them into the little van. He looked with admiration at Ernestine who wore white slacks, a white blouse, her favorite Italian sandals, dark sunglasses and a wide-brimmed cornflower blue hat. Her hair was neatly tucked under and only one unruly strand had escaped the confinement.

Ernestine was oblivious to his gaze and to her surroundings. Only one thing penetrated her whole being: Jonathan was gone forever. *He has left me and is never coming back.* Ernestine realized that she started to get angry at Jonathan for leaving her behind, hurting her so much that it was almost unbearable. She turned to Mary-Ann and in a sharp voice asked her:

"Where are you taking me? Don't think for one moment that I don't know what you are up to. You, you...," and Ernestine broke into tears. Mary-Ann took her into her arms and spoke softly to her.

"Shhh, my pet, you will be alright; time will heal your wounds as it does everybody's. It is good to be angry, have some emotions, and not be numb with grief. I am here for you for whatever you need me, be it as a friend or somebody you can vent your anger at. I will not leave you alone."

"I am so sorry, Mary-Ann. I don't know what came over me. I know you are doing this to help me, but it is so hard." Ernestine fell silent and contemplated the country-side. They were driving along the ocean toward Rio Grande where their hotel was located. After a little while longer, they arrived at their destination.

The hotel was situated among tall palm trees; red blooming bougainvilleas framed the entrance. In the open lobby, tall terracotta pots with red and white ginger were scattered randomly and gave the place an airy feel. Mary-Ann and Ernestine were led to their bungalow close by the water's edge.

The spacious living room was furnished with comfortable sofas and chairs in warm colors, overlooking the ocean. The large bedrooms with high ceilings were furnished with king beds, dressers and a small table with two chairs, all in white, even the thick curtains. The room had an air of muted elegance and luxury.

Mary-Ann and Ernestine unpacked their suitcases and placed their clothes in the dressers and closets. Then they went to explore their surroundings. From the lobby they had a view of the swimming pool and of the ocean beyond. They decided to go for a short walk on the beach. The day was warm but storm clouds were already gathering on the horizon.

"It will rain soon," said Mary-Ann, "but we have enough time for a stroll along the beach."

They walked in silence for several minutes, each one of them deep in thought.

"You know," said Ernestine, "this reminds me of the time I was walking with Jonathan along some beach in Hawaii. The sand was black and we were alone on that deserted beach. I don't remember where it was exactly but it was a place Jonathan knew and wanted to share with me."

Mary-Ann glanced at her and saw tears welling up in Ernestine's eyes. She noticed that Ernestine's eyes were the color of the ocean water, greenish-gray, and she suddenly understood why Jonathan had been captivated by these unusual color-changing eyes. She took Ernestine's hand and squeezed it.

"Let's go back and have something to eat in one of the hotel's restaurants," she said.

"I am not hungry," replied Ernestine.

"That's fine; but I am starving and could use your company. It's not much fun eating alone at a restaurant."

Ernestine had to smile. She understood what her friend was trying to do and she was going to let her. One miserable soul was enough.

They found a little restaurant tucked away in a corner of the hotel's property and ordered some chicken salad and a glass of white wine.

"Some dessert?" asked Mary-Ann. "I saw them pass by with some pastel de tres leches."

"I'd love some and some strong coffee with it."

Mary-Ann ordered the sweets and they savored the cake while chatting about this and that. Finally, it was time to leave and they ambled back to their bungalow. They bid each other a good night and went to their bedrooms.

Mary-Ann called Kevin on her cell phone and told him about the day.

"It went well. She is a strong woman and I hope that this will help her, at least for now. Eventually, she will have to face it that she is alone and that Jonathan will never come back to her. Tomorrow, we'll have some massages and maybe go swimming in the ocean, or just lay by the pool. Whatever Ernestine feels like doing. I want to make sure that as little as possible reminds her of Jonathan."

They talked a little while longer and then said goodbye. For a second, Mary-Ann thought she heard something outside her door and quickly went and opened it. But, only the empty living room was staring at her. She turned and closed the door.

Ernestine silently walked back to her bedroom and slipped under the sheets. They felt cool against her hot body. She tried to sleep but her mind could not find rest. Thoughts flooded in and seemed to overwhelm her. They jumped from events in the past to Jonathan's funeral. She turned on the bedside lamp and saw the pill Mary-Ann had left for her. She took it and swallowed it with a glass of water.

"I need to sleep," she thought, as the dark night embraced her.

Early the next morning, she was awakened by voices outside her bedroom door. She got up, donned a bathrobe and opened the door. She saw Mary-Ann arranging breakfast on the table, brought by room service. When she spotted Ernestine she smiled and said:

"Good morning. Come and have something to eat and a hot cup of coffee."

Ernestine went over to her, embraced her, and sat down at the table. There were fruits and juices, cereal and milk, yoghurts, bagels, cream cheese and a big pot of steaming coffee. Ernestine was not hungry at all, but she served some fruit and munched on a bagel. The black coffee tasted bitter but she did not mind.

Mary-Ann had arranged to have a full body massage in the morning and the afternoon they'd spend by the pool. Ernestine was glad that Mary-Ann took charge and the only thing required of her was to go along. She knew that these days were a reprieve from the dark days that were to come. She tried to put her fear aside and enjoy the sunny day.

The massage was wonderful. The skilled hands of the massage therapist were able to lessen the stiffness in her body and give her some comfort. Only too quickly was the time up and she had to walk back into reality.

Both women looked relaxed but Mary-Ann could detect the anxiety in Ernestine's eyes. They walked to the pool, read for a while, talked for a bit and went back to the bungalow to change for dinner.

Mary-Ann realized that it was best for Ernestine to stay at the hotel and so give her some semblance of a routine that felt soothing to her. The days went by quickly and it was soon time to pack and head back to the airport and to San Diego.

Kevin picked them up at the San Diego airport and they took Ernestine home.

"Do you want me to stay with you?" asked Mary-Ann.

"No, no, I am fine," replied Ernestine.

"In that case I'll look in on you tomorrow. Have a good night's sleep."

Kevin and Mary-Ann left and Ernestine stood alone in the apartment. She was wondering what to do next. Unpack? Go to sleep? Cry? She decided to go to sleep and deal with the world tomorrow.

Chapter 6
What Now, Ernestine?

A month had passed since that dreadful day when her life got shattered. She went through the days like a sleepwalker. She had no concept of time. She had to force herself to eat something, to shower every day; and she tried hard to function without Jonathan's love. Everything seemed so futile, every effort so meaningless.

"What's the point?" she would ask herself. I might as well be dead. I have no feelings left, no tears left to cry, no energy to undertake anything, and the future is just a never-ending chain of gray days, an alley shrouded in wet, icy fog. I am empty and have nothing left to give.

Sometimes she realized that she was wallowing in self-pity and that she had to make an effort if she wanted to avoid the gray fog that was gathering at the edge of her mind, and threatened to engulf her forever.

"I cannot let that happen," she would say aloud to herself. "I would lose Jonathan forever in this gray and frightening fog."

Slowly at first, she accepted her friends' invitations to meet them. They were all so very kind and considerate. But Ernestine understood that they could not feel what she was feeling, hard as they may try. Nobody knows what somebody else is feeling. Feelings are such a private part of human beings; they cannot be shared even with the people closest to you. Ernestine instinctively knew that she had to come to terms with her life on her own.

Kevin was the executor of Jonathan's estate and Ernestine was the sole heir to all of Jonathan's wealth. She was amazed at the extended holdings that Jonathan had. He had never really talked to her about this, nor about his childhood.

She knew that he was an only child and that his father was many years older than his mother. When once the untimely death of his mother came up, he told her that he had found his mother inside the running car in the closed garage. She was crying. Jonathan opened the door and helped her outside.

She told him not to tell anybody what he had seen and promised him not to do it again. So Jonathan did not tell his father about the incident. He did not want him to shout at his mother again. Jonathan kept his promise; but three months later his mother broke hers. This time she died and left eight-year-old Jonathan alone with his father.

"Jonathan," exclaimed Ernestine, "this is terrible. Did you tell anybody ever?"

"No, you are the first person I have told and please keep it to yourself."

"But Jonathan, it was not your fault, nothing to be ashamed of; you were just a little boy who believed his mother. You have carried this guilt with you all these years?"

"In the beginning it was terrible, but after the years went by it got easier. I just could not tell my father. It would not have accomplished anything. By the time I graduated from law school, it was in the distant past; and then soon thereafter, my father passed away."

"I don't know what to say. I am just so sorry you were left alone to deal with this," replied Ernestine with tears in her eyes.

Ernestine learned that she was a very wealthy widow. Jonathan had invested his money wisely and it had grown to a sizeable chunk of money. As there were no other heirs, the papers were signed quickly and Ernestine decided to take a trip to Easter Island, a place she had always wanted to visit.

Over the next few weeks she was busy arranging her trip. The day before her departure she invited her friends for some hors d'oeuvres, wine and drinks. They spent a lovely evening, and when they left they all wished her a safe trip.

Ernestine cleared up the kitchen and living room, made some last-minute preparations, and fell exhausted into bed. Sleep came quickly.

Sometime during the night, Ernestine woke up with a sharp pain in her abdomen. She was unable to move and the pain spread all over her body. She felt on fire, as if all her veins were filled with red hot lava. Breathing became difficult and she passed out. When she awoke again, the sun was high in the sky. She was thirsty and tried to get up, but fell back on the bed with a cry. Searing pain shot all over her body and she was about to pass out again. Only her will to stay conscious prevented her from fainting again.

"I have to get help; I need to call Mary-Ann." Slowly, she slid down from the bed to the cold marble floor and inched forward toward the little table where the antique phone was waiting for her. Every movement sent shivers of pain through her, threatening to make her faint again. She rested for a while and then inched forward again until she finally was able to reach the phone. She dialed Mary-Ann's number and when she answered whispered into the phone:

"Mary-Ann, help me; I cannot move."

"Ernestine, is that you? What are you talking about?"

But Ernestine was unable to say anymore. The pain that was engulfing her had taken over. Mary-Ann called Kevin and told him to meet her at Ernestine's apartment. Thirty minutes later, they were at Ernestine's door but she did not answer the door bell. Kevin went in search of the property manager while Mary-Ann stayed at the door.

When Kevin finally found the man, he asked him to open the door with the master key. The man was reluctant to do so but Kevin insisted. When the door was opened, Mary-Ann ran to the bedroom and found Ernestine unconscious on the floor. She immediately called for an ambulance and then checked her pulse.

"She is in real danger. Her pulse is racing and she has a high fever. We must get her to a hospital as soon as possible," she said to no one in particular. "I just hope we are not already too late."

Kevin just looked at her. He knew that his wife would not say something like that lightly. He rushed to the door and finally heard the elevator doors open and the paramedics appear with a stretcher. They gently lifted Ernestine onto the stretcher. Mary-Ann prepared the IV and then all of them headed down to the parking garage where the ambulance was waiting. With sirens howling and red lights flashing the ambulance headed to the Scripps Hospital in La Jolla, where Mary-Ann was working as a surgeon.

Ernestine was examined and they found that she suffered from a ruptured appendix. They did everything they could to prevent a deadly infection. After three hours in the operating room, Ernestine was wheeled to the intensive care unit where doctors and nurses monitored her vital signs.

Ernestine herself did not feel any of this. She was close to Jonathan and could not believe it when he told her that she had to go back to her body as her life was not yet finished.

Slowly, the nurse's voice penetrated the fog in Ernestine's brain and she tried to open her eyes. It took some effort but finally she looked at the face close to her and recognized Mary-Ann.

"Ernestine, wake up."

"I am getting there." Ernestine tried to smile. "Where am I?"

"You are in your room at the hospital," answered Mary-Ann and held her hand. "You are going to be just fine. We got to you in the nick of time and you should be out of here pretty soon."

"Thanks Mary-Ann," whispered Ernestine, and closed her eyes.

"Sleep; and I will look in on you later on."

Mary-Ann softly closed the door and Ernestine fell into a dreamless sleep and was awakened by voices in her room. Mary-Ann was trying to push someone out of the room but unsuccessfully. Ernestine recognized the man as an old friend of Jonathan's and called out to him.

"Eric, is that you?"

The tall bearded man turned around and came toward the bed. His hair was disheveled and his white shirt crumpled. The blue jeans hid a pair of well-formed legs, and his pudgy feet were stuck in a pair of brown sandals.

"Hi, Ernestine. How are you feeling?"

"Eric? Is that really you? Where do you come from?"

"Kevin called me; and Ernestine, I am so sorry about Jonathan. I was in the middle of the Amazon when I got the email. I could not get away immediately. So now, here I am. I drove down from Oregon as you can surely tell."

"Oh, Eric, it is good to see you, but I am not such good company right now. My whole body hurts and I am so sleepy. Maybe you could come back tomorrow, if you are staying around these parts, that is."

"Sure, I'll go take a shower and pass by tomorrow. Sleep well."

Eric left and Ernestine turned toward the wall. *When was it that I had seen Eric last?* she thought. But the answer was lost on her; sleep overcame her.

The next morning, Eric and Mary-Ann entered her room together ... Mary-Ann in her professional white uniform with the stethoscope hanging around her neck and Eric in clean slacks, red polo shirt and a huge bouquet of flowers in his arms.

"Hi, Ernestine!" they greeted her in unison. "How are you feeling this sunny morning?"

"I am feeling a lot better, but am still somewhat dizzy."

"This will pass, as the day goes on," answered Mary-Ann. "Let me take your vitals, and then I'll leave you two to your discussion."

"What discussion?" Ernestine wanted to know.

"I have a proposal for you," said Eric with a smile on his suntanned face. "I have talked it over with Mary-Ann and Kevin, and they think it is a great idea. Why don't you come with me to Oregon for a few weeks until you are healed? You need somebody to look after you, and I cannot leave Oregon at the moment; so come with me."

"I, I don't know," said Ernestine. "I need to think about this for a bit."

A nurse came into the room and took the flowers from Eric, put them into a tall vase that was standing on the window sill, and arranged them.

"These are beautiful blue irises, colorful freesias, and white roses!" she exclaimed, and put them on the table at Ernestine's bedside. She left the room and softly closed the door.

"I don't know, Eric. I would like to stay in San Diego rather than being up north. And what would I be doing all day? You'd be gone most of the time, no?"

"That's just it. I will be at my cabin for the next few weeks. I have to finish a project and would be with you most of the time. Now, I don't know if you could stand being with me for an extended period of time. It would be like in the old days, when I once stayed with you and Jonathan when I needed looking after."

Ernestine remembered the time Jonathan had come home with his rugged friend and introduced him as Eric, and taken him to the guest room.

"He'll stay with us for a while, Ernestine," he had said. "He's had some rough times and needs a place to recuperate. We've been friends since college even though his life took quite a different turn. He is an engineer and has worked for oil companies all over the world, sometimes in very dangerous countries. This last assignment brought him to the brink of a breakdown. As far as I could gather, he was tortured and witnessed some of his colleagues dying of the beatings."

"Of course; he's welcome to stay as long as need be."

So Eric stayed. Jonathan was able to refer some of his clients to junior staff and could spend more time with his long-time friend. They went sailing at the crack of dawn and it seemed that the sea air did wonders for Eric. Whether he ever told Jonathan about what happened at the camp, Ernestine never knew. She figured that if Jonathan wanted her to know, he'd tell her.

After two months, Eric felt restless and they had to let him go. He promised to stay in touch, a promise he had kept since the day he made it. Over the years, they received postcards from faraway places with some short information about how he was doing.

Once in a while, there would be a phone call from the airport asking them to join him for dinner at some restaurant or other in San Diego. Sometimes, he'd stay overnight or for a long weekend. He was always very polite and Ernestine knew instinctively that there was a very strong bond between these two unlikely men – one handsome, blond and blue-eyed, and the other dark with a somber look in his brooding dark eyes. One dressed for the sunny side of life and the other dressed as if he lived in some back alley.

Ernestine did not feel like going with this somber man whom she hardly knew. Yet, she could feel that he was serious about her staying with him and she also knew deep in her heart that she could not face staying in her four walls alone, remembering Jonathan every waking moment.

"Let me talk with Mary-Ann and I'll let you know tonight, okay?"

"Great; I'll see you tonight." And he left the room.

Ernestine looked up at the peach-colored ceiling and wondered what she should do. She realized that now that Jonathan was gone, she had to make this decision and all other decisions herself. How difficult this was. Jonathan had always known what to do.

She tried to picture the Oregon coast with its stony beaches, dark skies, and cold rain. It was not exactly an inviting picture. She tried to imagine the countryside; but before she got there, she fell into a drugged sleep.

Ernestine dreamed about her grandparents' house in England, but the surroundings were different. The house was perched on a steep cliff, the wind was howling, and the dark sea was bruising the rocks below. Ernestine stood at the edge and looked down into the swirling black water when suddenly a face appeared. It was Jonathan's face, distorted in an animal mask with bloody fangs, eyes glittering malevolently and from his mouth erupted a blood-curdling scream. Ernestine woke up with a start and found herself in her bright and sunny hospital room; Mary-Ann sitting on her bed with her arms around her.

"You had a bad dream, my pet," said Mary-Ann, wiping the sweat off Ernestine's face. "I heard you scream just as I passed your door on my way to the cafeteria."

"It was Jonathan's face that frightened me. It was horrid to look at," whispered Ernestine. "What does it mean?"

"It does not mean a thing," replied Mary-Ann. "It was a feverish dream and they distort reality."

"I guess you are right, but it leaves me with a funny feeling all the same."

"Forget about it. Can I bring you something from the cafeteria?"

"No thanks; but if you have time, could you come back and help me decide what to do about Eric, please?"

"Sure. See you in a while."

With these words, Mary-Ann left and Ernestine was left alone to brood over her strange dream. By now, the intensity of the fear she had felt was ebbing and she had difficulties remembering the abominable face.

She looked at the wallpaper and traced the lines with her eyes. They look like rivers flowing to nowhere. Before Ernestine could finish her thought, Mary-Ann came back with a huge cup of tea on a blue tray and some cookies on a little plate.

"Want some?" she asked.

Ernestine declined and asked her what she thought about Eric and his invitation. Mary-Ann told her that Eric had talked to her and Kevin the night before and that the three of them had agreed that this might be a good idea. It would take Ernestine's mind off Jonathan as there was nothing to remind her of him up in Oregon.

The place seemed to be comfortable according to Eric's description and she would also have a car at her disposal. A cook comes in every day to prepare Eric's meals and a maid is at hand to keep the house in order.

"Do you know anything about Eric?" asked Ernestine.

"Actually not much, but Kevin has been his friend as long as Jonathan has. They met in college and have stayed in contact all these years. He seems to be a chap one can count on."

"Funny," replied Ernestine, "that is what Jonathan told me too."

"You want to hear my opinion?" asked Mary-Ann.

"Go ahead."

"I think it would be a great opportunity for you to get away from your place, see something else, and try to figure out what you want to do with the rest of your life. On top of that, if you have enough you just come back. It's not like you are being held prisoner there."

Ernestine had to laugh and agreed that she would accept Eric's invitation and go to Oregon for a few weeks. Maybe it was true that it would do her good to get away … to try and hope again, after hope had become so elusive.

Something she once read and had stayed with her all these years came to her mind. She had seen it somewhere but she did not remember where, only that it had been written by Emily Dickinson. "Hope is the thing with feathers that perches in the soul, and sings the tune without the words, and never stops at all."

When evening came, Eric walked through her door with a big smile on his dark face. His brown eyes looked at her with warmth and he said:

"I heard that you have made up your mind? What have you decided, Ernestine?"

"I would very much like to come and stay with you for a while. I think it would be good for me to get away from here."

"It is settled then, as soon as you are discharged I will come and get you and take you with me. Mary-Ann told me that she would like to keep you here for a few more days, which suits me fine. I have some things to take care of in Los Angeles and then I'll come down here to pick you up."

Ernestine agreed and they talked about the things she should take with her which Mary-Ann and Kevin would pick up at the apartment for her. She protested as this meant that she would not go back to her own place, but Eric insisted it would be better for her to let Mary-Ann and Kevin take care of that. They would also look after the place while she was away.

Ernestine realized that she actually did not want to go back to 100 Harbor Drive right now. The pain was just below the surface and in order to get better she needed to leave it there.

"Tell you what," Eric said. "Write down all the things you need and it will be like going shopping for Mary-Ann. She will not have to worry about what you might like to take with you."

"Excellent idea and she can always call me if she is unsure."

So that was settled and Eric asked her to tell him about her day at the hospital. Ernestine started to talk and realized that it was very easy to talk to this big tough man. There was a gentleness about him that she had never before seen and she knew that she had made the right decision to go with him. When the night nurse came in, Eric got up, bid Ernestine a good night and left.

"He is one big guy," said the night nurse. "I would not like to get into a fight with him in a dark alley."

"I agree with you," replied Ernestine. "And could you give me something so I can sleep through the night, please?"

"Of course; I'll be right back," she said and went to bring Ernestine a sleeping pill.

Chapter 7
On the Road

A few days later, the morning saw Ernestine all dressed and ready to leave the hospital. She was sitting on the bed and looking out the window, marveling at the swaying palm trees and the little gray squirrels jumping around searching for food. Her heart was heavy and tears were rolling down her cheeks. There was such longing in her soul, such searing pain that she wished she could die and be once again together with her beloved Jonathan.

Footsteps were approaching her door and she quickly wiped away the tears and put on a smile when the door opened and Eric stood in the door frame.

"Ready?" he asked.

"Yes," Ernestine answered, trying hard to put some light tone into her voice.

"Give me your things and I'll take them to the car. Mary-Ann wants to say good-bye to you. I'll meet you outside, okay?"

Ernestine nodded and followed him into the corridor. Mary-Ann came toward her with outstretched arms and embraced her.

"Be happy, my pet, and let time heal your wounds. And remember, I am only a phone call away.

Ernestine hugged her and thanked her for all she had done for her. Then, abruptly she turned and quickly walked to the exit and Eric. He put her last suitcase into the back of the car and held the door open for her.

"Is there anything else you want to pick up from the apartment?"

"No, let's just go and be on our way."

Eric looked at her and understood that this was very difficult for Ernestine. Leaving with him was almost more than she could bear. Her face was still. Only her eyes seemed a bottomless ocean of shadows and sunlight. Her lips were slightly parted, and her breathing was labored. He closed her door, walked around the car, and sat behind the steering wheel. While pulling away from the curb he waved to Mary-Ann and then they were on Interstate 5, driving toward Oregon and a new life for Ernestine.

They did not talk much, and Ernestine seemed lost in her thoughts. Eric had turned off the interstate and was now driving along Pacific Highway with its spectacular views of the vast blue ocean stretching as far as the eyes can see. On the one side were precipitous cliffs that seem to fall into the churning waters below, and on the other side tall trees and dry-looking shrubs were running up a steep hill trying to reach the sky above.

The narrow road wound its way along the coast, crossing the tall Bixby Bridge, where an imposing viewpoint invited travelers to stop and take in the unparalleled view, before it led inland for a while, only to go back to the ocean as if pulled to the coast's edge by an unseen force. Ernestine was oblivious to all that and was staring straight ahead with unseeing eyes.

From time to time, Eric glanced at her and wondered what she was thinking. He found it amazing that this woman had decided to come with him and stay with him for a while. He figured that Jonathan's death had shaken her to her core and that something within her had broken and could never be healed again.

Some events were meant to change a person profoundly and he assumed correctly that this was what he was witnessing. A saying by Kahlil Gibran came to his mind: "Ever has it been that love knows not its own depth until the hour of separation."

"Let's stop and have a bite to eat. I am hungry," said Eric, and pulled into the parking lot of a small restaurant perched at the edge of a cliff. They ordered a couple of burgers with fries and a tall glass of lemonade for

Ernestine. The burger was delicious and Ernestine realized that she was actually hungry.

She looked at Eric who was talking on his BlackBerry. He was handsome, with his dark hair circling his head, chin set, and his eyes fixed to a point somewhere above the gray ocean waves. Suddenly, he turned as if he had become aware of Ernestine's gaze, and looked straight into her huge green eyes.

"Burger okay?" he asked.

"Very good," she answered. "I am really hungry and this is the perfect place to stop and rest for a while."

They finished their meal and strolled to the edge of the cliff. Looking about her, Eric started to tell her the history of the Pacific Coast Highway. Ernestine remembered having seen a documentary on TV about the expansion of roads along the Pacific coast and the difficult obstacles that had to be overcome by the construction crews. But American ingenuity had prevailed and today this is one of the most scenic drives.

"Wasn't there something called the Devil's Slide?" she asked.

"Yes, it's between Pacifica and Half Moon Bay. We should be there shortly."

After a while they returned to the car and took to the road again. Eric put on some light music and Ernestine quietly fell asleep. It was an uneasy sleep. She dreamed about Jonathan and the time he had to go to London for a couple of weeks.

She remembered how listless she had felt and that not even the blue sky and sunny weather could stimulate her into doing anything. She had sat listlessly in her favorite chair on the balcony looking at the sailboats with their sails flapping in the slight ocean breeze. Her heart was heavy and tears were rolling down her cheeks. She woke up when a hand gently touched her face.

"You were crying in your sleep," Eric said.

"I dreamed of Jonathan," she answered simply.

They were silent for a long while, each of them deep in their own thoughts. The landscape became more rugged and Eric was concentrating on driving with as few movements as possible.

"He is actually an excellent driver," Ernestine thought and watched the road curve and twist along the coast. This long drive so soon after her hospital stay was tiring and her bones seemed to hurt. A dreamless sleep took her pain away; and when she awoke, Eric had stopped at a quaint inn in Monterey. He helped her to her room on the top floor and put her little traveling case on the bed.

"When you are rested, let me know and we can go for dinner. There is a nice restaurant in Cannery Row and I am sure you'd like to visit some of Steinbeck's places that have become famous through his novels, no?"

"I'd love that," she answered. "I will just freshen up a bit and meet you in the lobby in about ten minutes, okay?"

"See you then."

He turned and left the room. Ernestine took a quick shower and donned a little dress she had Mary Ann pack for just such an occasion. It was made of green-blue silk and highlighted the color of her eyes. In no time, she was downstairs and they went in search of the little restaurant somewhere on Cannery Row.

"According to Steinbeck's novel, Bear Flag Restaurant used to be Dora Flood's whorehouse," said Eric. "Have you read *Cannery Row*?"

"Yes I did, many years ago, but I might read it again now that I have visited the actual place."

They finally found the restaurant, squeezed in among shops and other eateries.

"I believe Captain Bullwhacker's Restaurant is the one I am looking for," said Eric. "Let's try it anyway."

They entered a dark entryway that lead to a big dining room.

The tables sported red-and-white checkered tablecloths and rickety old chairs. The wooden walls were dark and the little lacy curtains on the windows had yellowed over time. A fresh little bouquet of flowers on each table gave the establishment a cozy feel. Ernestine and Eric sat down by a window overlooking Cannery Row. They ordered some sandwiches and sodas and ate in silence.

"I did not realize that I was so hungry," said Ernestine. "We just ate a little while ago didn't we?"

"Well it was over four hours ago and you did not really eat anything, unless you call fumbling in your plate eating," smiled Eric.

Ernestine was astonished at how easy it was to talk to this man. Of course, she had known him for a number of years, but she always regarded him as Jonathan's friend and not necessarily hers. Yet, here she was feeling safe and secure in his presence.

"... what do you think?" Eric asked.

"Sorry; what do I think about what?"

"Shall we go for a stroll along colorful Cannery Row before we head back to the inn?"

"Sure, let's do that," and Ernestine got up and grabbed her bag. Eric opened the door for her and they stepped into the famous street. Eric pointed out buildings from Steinbeck's novel and the now-defunct sardine factories. They looked out upon the cold water and slowly headed back to the inn. Freshly-baked chocolate chip cookies and milk in a porcelain jar awaited them on the buffet.

"I think I am going to indulge and take some with me upstairs," said Ernestine. "I cannot resist the sweet smell of these delicacies."

She put two cookies on a little plate, filled a glass with milk, and headed for the stairs.

"Good night Eric. I'll see you in the morning. I will be downstairs by eight o'clock, if that is not too late for you?"

"That is just fine. Sleep well, and I'll see you tomorrow morning for breakfast."

Ernestine climbed the stairs and opened the door to her room. On the center table stood a vase filled with white lilies and a little card protruded from the flowers.

"Thanks for your trust and your company, Eric."

Ernestine stared at the card and at the flowers. Their scent filled the room and made her slightly dizzy. Ernestine felt a thought wanting to intrude but she was too tired to concentrate. She put the cookies on her nightstand and slowly drank the milk from her glass, staring through the open window at the starry night.

The thought seemed to pound in her head and Ernestine decided to go to sleep. The moment she closed her eyes and sleep seemed to be within reach, the thought became as clear as crystal. Some years ago, Jonathan had surprised her with a weekend at Big Bear Lake.

They had driven up the mountain and had stayed at a small inn close by the lake. When she had opened the door to their cabin, the smell of lilies had enveloped her. On the center table stood a vase with white lilies and a little card by Jonathan. "I'll love you always," it had said.

They had spent a wonderful two days there, swimming in the cool lake and hiking up to the old gold mine. Jonathan had bought her a small jewelry box inlaid with mother of pearl as a memento of that weekend.

Ernestine felt tears running down her cheeks and her heart was heavy with sorrow. She missed Jonathan terribly and the longing for him was almost unbearable. Ernestine forced herself to think of something else, but her thoughts had a mind of their own and returned to Jonathan.

"My dearest husband," Ernestine whispered. "What am I to do without you? I am like a boat thrown around by giant waves, no land in sight and no safe harbor. You were the place where I had anchored my boat and intended to stay forever. But fate decided against that, and now I am drifting in an ocean of sorrow and tears. Blind to any rays of hope. Please my dearest man, if you can hear me, come to me in my dreams and show me a way."

The bright morning sun shone on Ernestine's face and woke her. The sky was an amazing blue and the water in the bay glittered like a thousand fiery diamonds. Ernestine showered, dressed, packed and went downstairs in search of breakfast. The lovely smell of freshly-brewed coffee led the way.

She found herself on a small terrace with white rattan chairs and glass-topped tables. Eric was already seated and waved to her. The sight of him gave her pleasure and she approached him with rapid steps.

"Did you sleep well?" he asked.

"I think so," although I had such a vivid dream; but it is gone now and only a feeling remains."

Eric looked questioningly at her with his currant-dark eyes.

"Care to elaborate?"

"Not now. It is such a beautiful morning. Let's enjoy our breakfast without any thoughts of yesterday."

Eric fell silent and attacked his scrambled eggs. Ernestine had ordered Eggs Benedict and was savoring every bite of it.

"This is my favorite breakfast," she told him. "Whenever it is offered somewhere, I order it. I am actually quite an expert on Eggs Benedict."

She smiled at him and her eyes shone with pleasure. Eric quickly looked down in search of his fork. He could not understand the feelings that washed over him. It had started last night when they came back to the inn and he had watched her putting the cookies on a plate and pouring herself a glass of milk. She then had said good night to him and had gone upstairs.

Her vulnerability had appealed to his basic maleness. She needed protection and he was here to do exactly that.

Protect her and serve her. He realized now that he would go to the ends of the world for her. But he also knew that Ernestine must never know his feelings for her. She would leave him in a heartbeat.

She had married Jonathan out of a deep and unending love and she would never be free again to love anybody else, nor would she want to. He still marveled at her decision to come with him; but then, she regarded him as Jonathan's friend and, therefore, he was her friend too and nothing more. For her, he was safe to be with. He would never insult Jonathan's memory.

After breakfast, they took to the road again and continued toward San Francisco.

"Do you want to stop at the Golden Gate?" Eric asked.

"Not really. We can drive on. I have been here many times with Jonathan," she answered.

Eric drove on and after a few hours they crossed into Oregon. The landscape had changed and the coast line had become more rugged. Huge waves pounded the silent rocks, and dark clouds gathered on the horizon. Ernestine watched the unfamiliar landscape pass by; and before she realized it, she had fallen asleep.

Chapter 8
The Log Cabin

A bump in the road awakened her unceremoniously.

"Had a good sleep?" Eric laughingly asked.

"Yes I did, and this time without any dreams," Ernestine answered. "Where are we?"

"About five miles from home. Hold on to your seat because the road is going to be rocky and very narrow, but we should arrive at the house in about twenty minutes."

Ernestine looked around her and what she saw pleased her eyes. Beautiful redwood trees were lining the road, curious ferns peeked out from the brush, and here and there a bright flower was trying to attract some sunlight. Suddenly, the forest gave way to a wide meadow bordering a deep blue lake. A weatherworn log cabin was perched on high ... a steep cliff to one side and pine trees on the other standing guard like soldiers.

Ernestine gasped. "This is breathtaking. However did you find this jewel?"

"I bought it some years ago from a friend who needed to sell it. It looks nice from the outside but the inside is old and could use some improvements. But I am so rarely here for any length of time that I don't get much done. However, I brought some tools with me and I hope I can fix some of the most pressing problems. I hope you are not disappointed."

"It is absolutely charming the way it sits by the edge of the water. Did you know that I have always dreamed of living in a log cabin? It seemed to me to allow for a much slower pace than anywhere else. Oh Eric, thank you so much for bringing me here."

"Wait with the thanks until you see the inside. I am afraid I haven't been up here in quite awhile and I suppose it needs some cleaning before we can install ourselves here."

"Don't worry, we can do it."

They entered the dark cabin and Ernestine was able to make out some furniture covered by huge sheets, a brick fireplace, and a kitchen at the end of the room.

"Let's open the shutters and let the sunlight in!" exclaimed Ernestine, and threw open the nearest window and its shutters. Sunlight flooded in and illuminated the big room. As they opened more windows and shutters, Ernestine looked about her and took off the sheets from the furniture. The sofa was green and red checkered with some black lines; the two chairs that matched were pulled up to the ceiling-high brick fireplace where firewood was ready to be lit in the hearth.

A thick, grayish pelt was draped over one of the arms of the armchair, and a colored bowl filled with nuts was standing on the little wooden coffee table. Woolen rugs covered the bare wood floors, and lace curtains gently moved in the warm breeze blowing from the lake. On the mantelpiece several candles stood at attention like toy soldiers, and a small box of matches was ready to be used. On the hooks behind the door, Ernestine saw some rubber coats hanging and the matching hats.

"You go fishing in these clothes?"

"No," laughed Eric. "They are used to get wood in the rain and snow."

But Ernestine had not waited for his answer. She had found a door leading upstairs and was eagerly climbing the steep stairs. On top of the stairs, several doors seemed to lead to treasures yet to be uncovered. Carefully, Ernestine opened the door to her right and found herself in a spacious office, complete with desk, chair, computer, telephone and a copier/fax/printer machine.

"Do you work from here?" she called to Eric. "This is a great office with the view of the forest and the garden below."

Eric had silently come upstairs and was standing behind her. He could smell her hair and her face cream. He imagined for a second what it would be like to hold her in his arms; but before he had thought the thought to the end, Ernestine turned and looked straight at him, her eyes shining bright in the pale light, and he took a step back.

Ernestine did not seem to notice his sudden shyness as she continued to bombard him with questions about the cabin. She opened the next door and found herself in a cozy sitting room with its own wood-burning fireplace. Again the chairs had been covered by big sheets which she now took off. This room sported two oversized chairs with a coffee table between them.

Large windows opened onto a small balcony overlooking the garden; and in the background a snow-covered peak could be seen. In the far corner, a daybed with lots of teddy bears stood along the wall. A huge armoire with colorful flowers painted on the door completed the room.

"Whose teddy bears are these?' asked Ernestine.

"They belonged to my friend's daughter," replied Eric, "and when they moved out they left them behind. This room was actually her bedroom and I kept it the way she left it."

Ernestine looked thoughtfully at Eric.

"You loved her?"

"Yes," was the short answer, and Ernestine felt that she had no business asking more questions about that girl. It seemed to touch a raw nerve in Eric.

"Maybe one day he'll tell me," she thought, "and if not it does not matter."

The next door she opened led to a modern bathroom, complete with a garden tub, walk-in shower, and lots of counter space. There was even a linen closet filled with towels and accessories.

"This is marvelous!" exclaimed Ernestine. "You've got yourself quite a place here."

She then went to the other side of the landing and opened a double door. The sunlight streamed through the large windows and made the dust specks dance. After pulling off the sheets covering most of the furniture in the room, Ernestine was silent. She turned to Eric and simply said:

"This is the most gorgeous and tasteful room in the house."

A large bed was placed against the wall to allow for a view of the blue lake. On the left was a fireplace with two chairs upholstered in a teal and yellow fabric matching the curtains and bedspread. Soft, silvery lace curtains gently moved in the breeze and little pillows were strewn all over the place. A door led to the large balcony where a hot tub was covered with a tarp. Eric took it off and checked the water.

"Let's ready it so we can soak our tired bones in it tonight."

Ernestine did not hear him as she had wandered into the bathroom that was just off the bedroom. It was large with white marble floors, walls and countertops. Huge gilded mirrors hung over the sinks and a round Jacuzzi invited one to stay for a while. A huge skylight spanned over it. Ernestine went back to Eric and found him fiddling with the hot tub.

"This is a very beautiful home you have here," she said. "How come, Jonathan never said anything about it?"

"He was never here. I travelled so much that when I came here I did not want to entertain. This was my very private place, shielding me from the world and everybody in it."

"I am very happy that you decided to share this place with me, at least for a while," Ernestine smiled.

Eric had to restrain himself. He felt like grabbing her and kissing her all over.

"What is happening to me?" he thought. "I'm behaving like a schoolboy with his first love. I have known and loved women more gorgeous than Ernestine, yet there is something about her that makes me want her the way I have never wanted any woman."

Abruptly he turned and went down the stairs.

"You can have the big bedroom," he called to Ernestine. "I will be perfectly fine in the teddy-bear room."

He went to the car and brought the suitcases upstairs, putting his in the teddy room and Ernestine's into the big bedroom. She protested, but he insisted on her having the great room.

Ernestine started to unpack her suitcase, putting her personal things into the dresser drawers and hanging her dresses, slacks, and blouses in the cedar armoire. She stopped for a second and looked out the window at the gorgeous view. The lake lay still like a mirror and she could see the clouds gathering in the west.

She stepped out onto the balcony and lifted her eyes up to the sky. "Oh Jonathan," she whispered, "where are you? Why did you leave me here all alone to fend for myself? I wish for nothing else than to be with you wherever you are."

A young bird was chirping nearby, calling for its mother to feed him and Ernestine instinctively knew that life was not going to grant her wish and that she had to master the rest of her life without her beloved Jonathan. She tried to pierce the clouds to see beyond them, to see the place where she imagined the departed souls gather after they have shed their earthly mantle.

She firmly believed that at one time she had seen this place, the day she flew to her parents' funeral. The airplane had crossed the clouds and cruised among strange cloud formations. It was like a big hall with clouds as white pillars and mist hanging between them like some eerie curtains.

Looking out of the window, Ernestine had felt such peace as she had not felt before. She had heard soft music playing and something soft had seemed to caress her cheek. She had wished she could stay in this lofty paradise; but then suddenly, the plane had veered to the left and descended toward the earth. However, the sensation of that incident stayed with her henceforth; and whenever she thought about it, peace filled her heart.

"Funny," she thought, "this is the first time since Jonathan's death that I thought of this place. Why did this not occur to me before?" Ernestine was convinced that this was a sign from Jonathan and that he wished her to be at peace with herself and the world.

"I will work on it, my love," Ernestine whispered and returned to the room and to the unpacking of her belongings.

When she was done, she sat down on the bed and looked around.

"I can certainly live here for a bit," she said to herself. She pulled up her feet, laid back on the pillows; and before she knew it, she had fallen asleep.

A gentle knock on the door woke her up.

"Ernestine, are you alright?" Eric's voice called to her.

She got up, opened the door and said:

"I fell asleep for a while but now I am hungry. Do you have anything in the kitchen that I can cook us a meal with?"

"Some frozen stuff is in the freezer; but I am afraid I have no idea what there is. Let's go and have a look. Hopefully we'll find something so we can postpone grocery shopping until tomorrow."

They made their way to the roomy kitchen and Eric opened the freezer. He stood there gazing at its contents. "Help, Ernestine!"

She gently pushed him aside and found some frozen chicken breasts, vegetables, and even fresh fettuccine.

"Let's stir-fry some of these things and we'll have a dinner fit for royalty," she smiled.

While Ernestine was preparing dinner, Eric sat at the island, drinking a beer, watching her. He wondered what this woman was doing to him. He wanted her, that much he knew but he also knew that if he was not careful and she found him out, she'd leave here immediately.

Her love for Jonathan was what kept her going and if that silver thread were ever broken, she'd float away into a world of her own. He knew that she needed time, probably more than he could reasonably give her, but he still heard Mary-Ann's warning in his ears:

"Eric, Ernestine's state of mind is very fragile. Any undue emotion could send her over the edge, maybe forever. Please treat her gently and do not make any passes at her. I know she is a desirable woman, especially now in her vulnerability, but you must refrain from letting her ever see any feelings for her. If it becomes too much, go away for a bit, she'll be able to cope without you, if she knows you will return as a good friend would."

Eric knew that Mary-Ann had hit the nail on the head. He was falling for Ernestine in a big way. Not having been one to disguise his feelings for the opposite sex, he now found himself in unchartered territory.

"I must be patient. Maybe slowly I will be able to conquer her, to maybe dim in her mind Jonathan's image."

He continued his reverie while Ernestine was clattering with pots and pans. After only a few minutes she exclaimed, "Dinner is served!"

They sat down at the little round table by the bay window. A checkered tablecloth covered the table and two plates with steaming food were waiting. She had arranged the seating so that both could look out and watch the sun set over the trees.

"This is excellent!" exclaimed Eric. "I usually do not eat such exotic meals."

"It is a recipe that I once found in an old cookbook. It is easy to make with almost any ingredients. And depending on the spices at hand it tastes different every time. I am glad you like it."

They both dug into their food and ate silently. The western sky put on a splendid show of different colors; and when the sun finally disappeared behind the trees, Eric turned on a small lamp that bathed the room in a warm glow.

They took the dishes to the sink and returned to the living room, stretching their legs in front of the fireplace. They talked for a while about their trip and what needed to be done tomorrow.

A little later they went upstairs and each entered their own room. Ernestine did not even think about it, but Eric could not put the thoughts out of his mind. When he finally fell asleep he was tormented by dreams of Ernestine.

The next morning, Ernestine woke up when the sun was shining into her room. She jumped out of bed, put on her dressing gown and traipsed downstairs. The delicious smell of freshly-brewed coffee greeted her, and Eric was busy at the stove.

"Good morning," she said and looked into the frying pan where Eric was stirring eggs, tomatoes, onions and bacon. "This smells great. May I have some, please?"

"Of course. I made this especially for you. It is my secret recipe," he smiled.

He served her a generous portion, poured the black, hot coffee into a sky-blue mug, and brought it to the wooden table.

"Enjoy!" He leaned back in his chair and observed her eating. After breakfast, Eric showed her the surrounding meadows and creeks where he would go for long walks to think things through. Back at the house, they jumped into the car and drove to town to buy some groceries.

The little general store carried a variety of staple foods, fresh fruit and vegetables, and they bought what they thought they needed. Lettuce from the Salinas Valley, apples grown in Washington, ripe bananas from some faraway place, and noodles made fresh daily by a local family, as well as locally-grown vegetables of all sorts.

They laughed while putting their treasures into the back of the car and decided to take a quick look at the town before heading back.

There was a small craft store, a bank, a pharmacy and some curio stores that were visited by weekend tourists during the summer. Ernestine was delighted to live close to this small town where life had a different pace.

The days following their shopping trip were spent with long walks along the blue lake or through the green forest, cooking together, watching the sunset from the porch and reading by the fireplace. Eric and Ernestine had found a routine that was easy and non-threatening, at least for Ernestine. She was oblivious to Eric's inner turmoil. The days turned into weeks and fall was approaching when Eric told her one morning:

"I have to leave for a couple of weeks. My presence is required in the Middle East. I leave this afternoon. You can stay here of course, and I will leave you the car so you can go into town. Sorry about the short notice."

His heart was heavy but he knew he had to save himself.

Ernestine looked at him and said:

"Don't worry, I will be fine. I think I will go into town and buy some painting supplies and try my hand at that. I have wanted to do this for so long."

Eric got up and went upstairs to pick up his suitcase. He had already packed, as he was in a hurry to get out of the house and away from Ernestine.

Chapter 9
Mary-Ann's Story

Ernestine drove into town and browsed the stores for her painting supplies. She quickly found what she wanted and returned to the house. It was still sunny but the day was ending and Ernestine got herself busy making dinner. While sitting down with her salad and chicken breast she felt all of a sudden very lonely. Tears stung her eyes and she put the dishes into the sink and went upstairs.

She pulled a few clothes into her blue overnight bag, ran down the stairs, locked the door and jumped into the car. She drove to the airport and bought a ticket to San Diego. She was lucky and made the last flight which would get to San Diego at 9:30 pm.

The flight was uneventful and she dozed most of the way. When the intercom came on telling them that they would be landing in about 20 minutes, Ernestine was happy.

She hailed a cab that brought her to her apartment. She took the elevator to her floor and opened the door. She saw light emanating from her bedroom and she tiptoed to the door and silently opened it a crack allowing her to peek into the room. What she saw startled her.

In her bed was Mary-Ann making love to some stranger. Her black hair was loose and she was moaning in ecstasy. Ernestine stood in the doorway looking in utter bewilderment at her friend. She did not know what to do. The situation was unbelievable. Ernestine was about to turn around when Mary-Ann spotted her. With a cry she stammered, "I can explain, Ernestine."

Ernestine fled into the living room and slumped into the big soft chair, Jonathan's chair. Memories began flooding her mind and she felt like a palm tree in a hurricane. She lost her bearings; and only when someone was shaking her and calling her name was she able to escape the memories.

"Ernestine, Ernestine, wake up!" Mary-Ann cried, "I am so sorry about this mess."

Ernestine opened her eyes and looked at her friend.

"What on earth are you doing, having sex with some stranger? What about Kevin? Don't you care about him anymore? What is going on?" Ernestine whispered.

"It is a long story; but in a nutshell I will try and explain."

Mary-Ann sat beside Ernestine on the chair, took a deep breath, and told her that about three years ago, Kevin had a boating accident and became impotent. They had been going from doctor to doctor, clinic to clinic, but nobody was able to help him. His condition was irreversible.

They loved one another and decided to stay together, that they would find a way to beat this thing. At the beginning it was fine. Mary-Ann had her work that kept her satisfied; but as time went by, she became increasingly irritable. She realized that she needed more than an occasional hand-induced orgasm, and she and Kevin decided that she should find somebody else.

However, Mary-Ann did not want a relationship with someone, only an occasional night full of raw sex. Kevin did not like the idea of her doing this but understood her needs needed to be taken care of. He arranged for men to meet her somewhere and to give her the satisfaction he was no longer able to give her.

Usually she would meet the men in a hotel room; but when Ernestine moved away with Eric they decided that it would be better if Mary-Ann would meet the men at Ernestine's place. It was more discreet and nobody would know.

"Now you know our secret. I beg you not to tell Kevin that you know. This situation is devastating enough for him. I don't know what he'd do if he knew that you know."

"I will not tell him, nor will I tell anybody else," replied Ernestine. "Did Jonathan know?"

"I couldn't say," whispered Mary-Ann. "After our initial discussion we have not talked about it anymore. It is too painful for both of us."

"I am so sorry for both of you and I wish that there was something that could be done," said Ernestine, and went to the kitchen to get a glass of cold water. Mary-Ann followed her.

"I will take the sheets off and wash them, which is what I usually do anyway."

With these words, Mary-Ann went back to the bedroom, removed the sheets and put on fresh ones. She tidied the room and opened the windows to let the fresh ocean breeze in.

"Where is the man?" Ernestine asked under the door.

"I told him to leave the moment I saw you standing there. I will not see him again," replied Mary-Ann.

The two women stared at one another across the bed and both knew that their friendship had irreversibly changed, but that with time and understanding a new friendship would evolve.

"What brought you here, Ernestine? I thought you liked the rugged Oregon coast?"

"Eric had to fly to the Middle East for a couple of weeks and I just decided to come home for a bit," replied Ernestine, "but I think I will return tomorrow morning. It makes no sense now for me to stay here. I need to understand what happened tonight before I can face you and Kevin. You understand, don't you?"

"Yes" said Mary-Ann, simply. "I thank you for it."

Mary-Ann left and Ernestine looked out the big picture window that overlooked the bay. Thoughts whirled in her head but she was unable to grasp a single coherent phrase. She turned off the lights and went to sleep on the couch. She could not bring herself to sleep in the bed so recently vacated by her friend and her lover.

An uneasy sleep overcame Ernestine and when she woke it was almost noon. The sun stood high in the sky and the shadows of the plants danced on the walls to music only they could hear. She watched them for a while. The futility of that dance seemed to mirror her own life. She realized that she had lost her bearings and was dancing aimlessly like the shadows on the wall.

She got up, straightened the sofa, and stepped on the balcony. The ocean breeze felt good on her face and she sucked in the fresh air in big gulps. She went to the fridge and served herself a tall glass of lemonade that Mary-Ann had made. "Funny," Ernestine thought. "Here I am, alone, Jonathan gone forever; and yet, I think I have it better than Mary-Ann. She must feel so guilty and yet unable to help it. Going home last night and looking into Kevin's eyes as if nothing had happened. Even worse, he knows, as he usually arranges these meetings to save Mary-Ann from the humiliation of finding dates. I wonder if they talk about it. Well, I will never know that. It is none of my business."

Finishing her lemonade, Ernestine went back into the apartment to find some clothes and to take a shower. It felt good to be home again and she decided to stay and have her things shipped from Eric's place. The warm water ran down her face and she actually felt happy. Then emotions hit her like a wet cloth and she started to cry.

"Get ahold of yourself!" said the little voice in her head. "There is nothing wrong with feeling happy. It is the normal state of human beings. If only they would accept it and not think that they have to run after happiness which they most often mistake for money, and more money."

"I shall heed your words," said she to herself, and stepped out of the shower. The white towel was very soft and she vigorously dried herself and her hair. She walked to her closet and chose a green dress with butterflies that offset her long red hair. On the way out, she put on her favorite sandals.

She had decided to walk to Seaport Village and watch the world pass by on one of the benches facing Coronado. On the way there, she bought herself a hamburger and some fries as a treat and sat down on a bench munching her lunch. It was a warm day and many people were out for a stroll, eating their lunch while enjoying the breeze before they headed back to their offices.

Ernestine watched the small ferry come and go, listened to the musicians dressed in colorful clothes playing a spiffy tune to entertain the passersby, and smelled the popcorn popping in the red cart close by. When she had finished her burger, she strolled over to the merry-go-round, bought a ticket, and went for a ride on the white horse like Mary Poppins. While the horse went up and down, Ernestine thought how good it felt to be alive, and she started to make plans for her future.

When the horse finally stopped, she jumped off and felt years younger. She did not yet know what she was going to do but she knew that something had changed and that she was going to decide for herself where she was going in this one life she had been given. She remembered a good friend telling her once: "Don't forget, this is it, this is not a dress rehearsal!"

She walked back to the apartment. Her step had a spring in it that it had not had for some time. She watched the children play in the little park, marveled at the architecture of the Convention Center, and waved at the people in the red trolley.

The elevator took her to her apartment and, while she opened the door, she heard the phone ringing. She ran to the living room where her favorite white phone was standing in its charger. She picked it up but she was too late. The caller had hung up. She took off her shoes and hung her purse behind the door when the phone started to ring again. This time she answered at the second ring. Mary-Ann was at the other end of the line asking whether she could swing by later in the afternoon. Ernestine said yes and hung up. She was wondering what Mary-Ann wanted.

Around five o'clock, the doorbell rang and Mary-Ann stood there. Her hands were holding bags of Chinese food she had picked up on her way over.

"Hi, Ernestine. I thought we might as well have a bite to eat while I try and explain a few things to you. I only wish I had done it before."

"I am listening," said Ernestine while putting the food on little plates.

"Sit down here with me," said Mary-Ann, "and let's eat before I delve into the story of my life."

They silently nibbled at the food. After a few bites they put down their chopsticks and Mary-Ann began her tale.

She had been born into an Amish family living in Indiana. She grew up with three sisters and three brothers. They had to help their parents with the farm and the household chores. Life was good and they had many happy years.

But then her younger sister, Emma, became ill. By the time the village doctor told her parents that he could not do anything more for her and that it would be best to take her to the hospital, months had passed. Her parents arranged for a car to take her sister to the hospital in Indianapolis. A few days later, a friendly voice from the hospital called and told them that there was nothing they could do. She had a brain tumor and had only a few more weeks to live.

Mary-Ann and her parents hired a car and went to see her at the hospital. Mary-Ann was amazed at the hospital building. So many doors and windows; and when they entered it was like entering a different world. Nurses and doctors in their uniforms were hastening along the corridors, entering rooms with frowns on their faces, sometimes a smile when they came out.

The smell was very intriguing and Mary-Ann could not figure out what it was. They arrived at her sister's door and entered. Emma looked so small in the big hospital bed. Her skin looked gray compared to the white linen; and her big, dark eyes looked sad. Her beautiful black hair had been shaven, and her skull was gleaming in the sterile light of the room. Mary-Ann would never forget that sight.

It was decided that Mary-Ann would stay at the hospital with Emma and keep her company. During that stay, Mary-Ann got to know the doctors and nurses that cared for her sister and she decided that she was going to become a doctor so girls like Emma did not have to die so young.

The funeral was in the deep of winter, at the end of January. In the evening, Mary-Ann told her parents that she wanted to go to high school and then to college.

Her parents were flabbergasted. Amish children usually attended only elementary school and then learned a trade. There were some exceptions. Some boys had attended high school, even college, but girls?

Her father was furious and forbade her to even think about it. Her mother, however, talked to her and understood why Mary-Ann wanted to go to high school. She talked to her husband and he grudgingly agreed to let her attend high school. But that was it. No college. So Mary-Ann went to high school in the nearby town.

After graduation she presented her parents with the acceptance letters from various colleges. One of them was from UC Irvine – Medical College offering her a full scholarship. She informed her parents that she had already accepted their offer and was leaving for Irvine in the next few weeks.

Her father was beside himself with anger and her mother silently cried. The next day, her mother told her that her father did not want to see her ever again and that she had to leave their community. Her father had her shunned.

Mary-Ann could not believe it that she would have to leave without ever coming back. But her desire to study medicine was stronger than her father's hatred and she packed her few belongings in a suitcase and left without looking back at the house she grew up in.

She finally arrived at Irvine, found her dorm, enrolled in her classes, and waited for the semester to start. Her mother had given her some money to buy clothes and to tide her over until she got to Irvine.

Mary-Ann applied as clerk in a drug store and worked long hours without complaining. She kept to herself and when finally the day of the beginning of the semester came, she was very happy. She loved to study, the courses were of immense interest to her, and she excelled in any subject she chose.

Quickly, her academic abilities were brought to the attention of the head of the medical school. He took her under his wing and guided her through the storms and turbulences of life at the university. She graduated summa cum laude and was offered several residencies in various cities. She chose UCSD as she had liked San Diego the first time she visited this city.

While at UCSD, she met Kevin; and after a short courtship, they were engaged to be married. Mary-Ann invited her parents to the wedding but they declined. The wedding took place and she and Kevin found a small apartment where they were very happy together. Once they had finished with their studies, they bought a house and life seemed to be great.

They made plans about when and how many children to have, where to buy a vacation home, and they also made many friends. However, most of their friends were Kevin's friends from school or college whose wives then became friends of Mary-Ann. This shielded Mary-Ann from having to tell her sad story.

Jonathan also was a long-time friend of Kevin's, and when the two couples met they made a handsome little group. The guys would go sailing together and the girls would cook something delicious until the tired sailors came home. They spent many a happy hour together. But then all that changed the afternoon Kevin had his boating accident.

"I am so sorry," whispered Ernestine. "I had no idea what you had gone through."

"Nobody really does, except Kevin; and I ask you to please keep it to yourself."

"Why did you not ask for the use of the apartment?" I'd have let you use it any time," said Ernestine.

"No, we couldn't. How would you have reacted had we told you that it was to be my lovers den?" asked Mary-Ann.

Ernestine put her arms around Mary-Ann, held her tight, and said:

"Use the apartment whenever you need and I will call you before I come to San Diego, so you have time to make other arrangements, okay?"

"Thank you, my friend," said Mary-Ann, who then got up, took her purse and left.

Ernestine remained seated and contemplated the darkening sky. How strange and obscure our lives are. When we think we know our destiny, something happens to throw us off course. We also think we know the people we live with; and yet, everybody has something hidden away in a dark place deep inside.

When the sky had turned from blue to dark blue, and the first street lights started to shine their light onto the gray pavement, Ernestine got up, lit a few white candles, and closed the balcony door. She took the food to the kitchen and went back to sit down and think.

She understood that she had to do something with her time. Just letting the days pass without an aim seemed to be reckless. She felt reluctant to think about this, but forced herself to face this issue.

"Maybe I could work again," she mused but quickly abandoned the thought as she could not see herself being bound to a nine-to-five schedule again. She did not really want to interact with people, not just yet. She needed time, but time for what? All the many things she and Jonathan had planned to do in a few years were not going to happen. She could not bring herself to go anywhere without him.

She remembered when they had talked about renting a villa in Tuscany for a whole summer and live like artists, scouring the countryside for ideal places to paint, find little restaurants that only served common fare, and bicycle through the Tuscan hills.

Or maybe spend some time in the City of Lights, walking up to Sacre Coeur, watching the night fall and the lights go on, rummaging around Montmartre, and visiting the many museums Paris has to offer.

She recalled the many weekend trips they had planned which never materialized as there was always something more fun to do at home.

"Enough dreaming about things past," she reminded herself. "I really need to concentrate on what I want to do with my time." She opened a magazine that was lying on the coffee table and leafed through it. Her eyes got caught by an article about oil companies and that brought Eric to mind.

"I have to go back to Oregon and explain to Eric what I need to do. I cannot just have my things shipped here without facing him. He has been extremely kind to me without putting any claim to me."

Ernestine got up and booked a ticket to Portland for the next day. She went then to bed and slept until the morning sun kissed her cheek. She got up, showered, dressed and packed and was on her way to the airport when she received a call from Eric.

He had come home earlier than expected and was worried when he did not find her at the house. Ernestine told him that she was on her way to Portland and would arrive in a few hours. They agreed that he would pick her up at the airport. Ernestine dialed Mary-Ann's number and left her a message that she had returned to Oregon.

The flight was short but bumpy and Ernestine was glad when she could get off the plane. Eric was waiting for her with a bouquet of flowers in his arms.

"Welcome back," he smiled and guided her to the car.

"Thank you for picking me up and for the lovely flowers," Ernestine replied.

Somehow the silence between them felt good and they drove home without further conversations. At the house, Eric took Ernestine's blue overnight bag and carried it to her room.

"Thank you," said Ernestine. "I'll unpack later. I am hungry and could do with a bite to eat. What about you? Shall I make us some food?"

"That would actually be nice," replied Eric. "I am tired and am looking forward to an early night."

With these words he left her and went to his room. Ernestine was puzzled by his attitude but figured that he must be exhausted after this long drive and the long flight.

She went downstairs to the kitchen, looked into the fridge, and started to make some dinner for the two of them. When it was ready she went upstairs to tell Eric. But when she pushed the bedroom door open she saw him sprawled on the bed, fast asleep.

"I will let him sleep. This is more important than a meal," she said to herself and covered him with the blanket, closed the heavy curtains, and went downstairs, closing the door softly behind her.

Next morning they had a big breakfast and Eric told her the adventures of this last trip. The hours passed by quickly and before they realized it, the sun was standing high in the sky.

"But here I go, blabbering about my trip," said Eric. "Tell me, why did you go to San Diego?"

Ernestine did not have an answer and told him so. "It was one of those spur-of-the-moment decisions. To be perfectly honest, I could not face the prospect of being here all alone. And so I booked a flight to San Diego to sort out my life and find a purpose to being."

"And did you find a purpose?" Eric asked, with a twinkle in his gentle eyes.

"Not yet," Ernestine replied, "but sooner or later I will know," she replied purposefully.

Chapter 10
Tuesday

The days passed and Eric was fixing some windows that did not close properly when Ernestine heard a thud and Eric calling for her. She raced up the stairs and found him in the sitting room holding his hand, blood dripping to the floor. His face was ashen and covered in cold sweat.

"What happened?" Ernestine almost screamed, at the sight of so much blood.

"The window dropped down while my hand was still on the window sill and cut into my middle finger."

"Let's get you to a doctor or an emergency room. Is there something in town?"

Ernestine knew where the doctor's office was, as she had seen the sign when they had walked around town. She quickly called and was told to go directly to the hospital as the injury she described probably needed stitches.

Ernestine packed Eric into the car and drove to the hospital. Nurses were waiting and Eric was attended to without the long delay one usually experiences at the emergency room. After what seemed to Ernestine a very long time, the doctor and Eric appeared. Eric's hand was bandaged and some color had returned to his face.

"He needs some rest and antibiotics to prevent an infection. Have him come back in about seven days and I'll make sure the finger is healing nicely." With these words the doctor left them and went back to the emergency room to help the next patient.

"Does it hurt much?" Ernestine asked, concerned.

"Not much," Eric replied. "They gave me some painkillers and I got four stitches."

They walked silently to the car and drove home. Eric went upstairs to lie down for a while. When Ernestine looked in on him, he was sound asleep.

"He looks like a big baby," thought Ernestine, and smiled to herself. It is amazing how fragile we are. A little cut and we keep on bleeding; and if nothing is done to stop the bleeding, then life will just ebb away, like the day ebbs away when the sun is setting and night is coming. She walked downstairs and sat down in her favorite red chair.

She thought of Jonathan and how nothing could have been done to save him. His injuries were so grave that he died almost immediately. She vaguely remembered the police officer telling her that Jonathan's heart was pierced by a piece of metal sticking out from the other car.

Tears started to well up in her eyes and silently fell onto her folded hands. A rage filled her heart such as she had never known before and silently she cursed God and all his angels. "Where were you when Jonathan needed you most? Why did you have to let him die? He was too young and gentle and good to be taken from me in this way. Why could you not have taken us both on one of our trips together? Why him? And why do I have to live without him? I never wanted this. You are cruel; and for all I know you don't care about us at all, and all is just a tale of old."

She looked out of the bay window and to her surprise she saw the most beautiful rainbow she had ever seen, spanning the whole firmament. Its red, yellow, green, and mauve colors were vibrant, and it seemed as if God was answering her laments by showing her the immense beauty of nature, while a little voice inside her head was talking to her in a sweet voice.

"Stop it, stop it!" she cried out and covered her ears with both hands.

"What do you want me to stop?" asked Eric, walking down the stairs.

Ernestine quickly wiped her eyes with the sleeve of her blouse and turned to face him.

"Nothing at all. I was just quarreling with my fate," she replied with a forced smile.

"Do not stop on my account. I have something to pick up in the village and I will be back shortly."

With these words, Eric opened the door, started the car and drove off. Ernestine was completely taken by surprise.

"What did just happen?" she asked herself. "He has never left without asking whether I wanted to come along." Slowly, Ernestine turned around, closed the door, and went to the window. The rainbow had almost disappeared and the little voice in her head was quiet.

"What a strange day this is," she thought to herself, and went to the kitchen to see what she could make for dinner.

Suddenly, she heard the car drive up and heard Eric calling for her. She went to the front door and there, on the mat, sat the cutest little black Labrador puppy. It had a big red bow around his neck, and it looked at her with such trusting eyes that Ernestine had to pick it up and hold it close to her.

"Happy Tuesday," Eric smiled.

Ernestine was silent and she just looked from the puppy to Eric.

"It is for me?" she asked incredulously.

"Yep, just for you. I have more stuff in the trunk," Eric said. "Come help me unload."

Ernestine went to the car but did not let go of the puppy. Looking in the trunk, there was a bed for the puppy, food and food bowls, leashes, a blue collar with the license, and about ten different toys to play with.

"Oh Eric, I don't know what to say. This is marvelous to have a companion. You really care about me and know me very well, don't you?"

Ernestine did not wait for his answer and he answered her question silently: "If only you knew how much I care and how much I want to tell you this. But the time is not yet right and I have to be patient. Hopefully, one day soon I will be able to show you my true feelings without scaring you away. Until then, I have to keep my secret."

They carried all the fun things for the new puppy into the house and Ernestine busied herself to make a home for the frightened little dog.

"I'll call him Tuesday," Ernestine said suddenly. "You brought him home on a Tuesday and that shall be his name."

"Her name," Eric said.

"Oh, he is a she, that's splendid. Now we are two females against one male. You lose!" Ernestine laughed.

She went about the house with Tuesday and showed her where everything was. Eric heard her talking softly to the little pup and wondered if she would ever talk to him in that peculiar way of hers.

He realized that he had never seen her so happy since she had come with him to Oregon and was glad that he had finally made the decision to get a dog. With Ernestine at the house it would not be a problem if he had to go abroad for a while. He was sure Ernestine would take care of it.

The decision to give the puppy to her he had only made on the way back from town. He had been watching Ernestine from the landing and had seen her tears and how agitated she was. He could only guess that it had to do with Jonathan's death. Oh, how he longed to be able to take her in his arms, caress her and take this terrible hurt away. "My time will come," he thought.

Laughter came from the upstairs rooms and he quickly darted up the stairs to find Ernestine rolling on the floor with little Tuesday on her belly.

"She is so charming and trusting," Ernestine smiled, and looked up at Eric with her big green eyes so full of love and tenderness that he almost lost his composure. At the very last second he refrained from pulling her up and into his arms. It was almost too much to bear for him and he quickly knelt down to pick up Tuesday and help Ernestine to her feet. "Shall we go for a walk with Tuesday?" Ernestine asked.

"I think Tuesday has had enough excitement for one day. She is only a puppy and looks very sleepy to me."

"You are right." And with these words, Ernestine carried the little dog to her little round puppy bed; and even before she released her, Tuesday was fast asleep.

Sitting on the big sofa in the living room, Ernestine started to tell Eric about another black Labrador. Her grandparents in England had a dog called Winni when Ernestine was but a child. Winni was already ten years old at that time and was happy to just be around people.

She would still chase after Ernestine when she'd be out in the garden, but Winni tired quickly and would lie down on the cool grass under the big chestnut tree and take a nap. Ernestine would sneak up on her and pull her ears or tickle her nose with a blade of grass. Winni would just open her eyes and look about and fall right back to sleep. Ernestine recalled a picture of her and Winni where she had fallen asleep with the dog, and Grandma had quickly gotten the camera and taken a picture to capture that precious moment.

"I wonder where that picture is," mused Ernestine. "So many things get lost that are irreplaceable, when a home has to be cleared out."

"Maybe it is among your parents' things?" offered Eric.

"Could be. One of these days I will look through those boxes and crates and sort them out."

Her parents had died some five years ago in a plane crash near Halifax. They were on their way to England to visit with family. Ernestine remembered watching the evening news when an alert flashed on the screen informing the world that a flight had gone down into the waters off the coast of Halifax. It seemed to be a Swissair flight en route from New York to Geneva.

A dark and heavy feeling had spread through her and she quickly checked on the Web for her parents' flight. There was a notice that family members of passengers of flight SR111 should call the number listed. With dread, she dialed the number and listened to a recording, telling her that flight SR111 from New York to Geneva had been lost at sea and that further news would be broadcast as it became available.

She had immediately called Jonathan who was on his way home to be with her after he had heard the dreadful news on the radio. She remembered sitting with him on the sofa, watching the news and checking endlessly on the Web for any new developments.

Finally, close to morning, an announcement was made that unfortunately there seemed to be no survivors, that boats which were sent to the crash site had been unable to locate any survivors, and had only been able to recover some bodies the sea was willing to give up. Those bodies were taken to Halifax and family members were invited to come to Halifax.

Ernestine and Jonathan flew there the next day. The gym had been converted into a temporary morgue. It was a horrific sight. Black body bags neatly in rows, tearful people along the whitewashed walls, and flowers strewn all over the floor. The atmosphere was oppressive and Ernestine had to run out to get some fresh air and away from the ghastly sight.

Jonathan was looking for her parents but could not find them. Many passengers were kept by the sea, and her parents were among them. It was ironic that they should be buried at sea, the same sea they had so loved when they were alive.

There had been a funeral mass held at Peggy's Cove for the passengers buried at sea. It had all been very solemn and darkly beautiful. The white lighthouse with its red top standing erect like a soldier at attention gazing through cold mist toward the gray roily sea, the smooth rocks glistening with moisture, seagulls ebbing on the never-ending waves, and the forbidding heavy rain clouds ready to burst with icy rain.

Ernestine had thrown a bouquet of white and red roses into the sea and said her good-byes to her parents in their wet grave. She would never forget the day, September 2, when she had lost her beloved parents.

Ernestine did not remember how she got back to San Diego. Only that in the morning she awoke in her bed with Jonathan beside her. They had to go to her parents' house in Coronado and sort out things to keep, things to sell, and things to give away. It was a difficult task for Ernestine and she often thanked God for Jonathan who seemed to know what needed to be done and how to do these things.

There were important papers that needed to be sorted out, friends of her parents needed to be informed, the house readied for sale. It seemed an endless list of things that needed to be done. But eventually, it was all done and Ernestine was left to grieve. There were so many things she had wanted to ask her parents … about her childhood, their childhood, about relatives and friends, favorite recipes, favorite places to visit, what they liked or disliked.

But now it was too late. It was also too late to tell them how much she loved and cherished them. She was glad though that during their last dinner together she had told them that she loved them and was already looking forward to their coming home again. Little did she know then that this was the last time she would talk to them or see them alive.

"Are you okay, Ernestine?" asked Eric with concern in his voice.

"I was just thinking about my parents and all the things I wanted to ask them and now will never be able to ask," she whispered.

But right then, they both heard a loud yawn and some traipsing little feet coming toward them. Tuesday had awakened and was looking around trying to figure out where she was.

"Come here, little one," cried Ernestine, and Tuesday followed her voice. She stopped at her feet and looked up at Ernestine with her big, brown, trusting eyes. Ernestine bent down and scooped the puppy up in her arms and sat her in her lap.

"You are a soft little girl, aren't you?" she whispered into her ear. And Tuesday, as if she had understood, gave a short little bark in agreement.

Ernestine put Tuesday down, got up and went to the kitchen to fill Tuesday's stainless steel bowl with puppy food and water. Tuesday followed her and watched her every move. When the bowls were finally put in front of her she ate heartily.

After she had drunk some water, Ernestine took the leash from the hook behind the door and called Tuesday. "Come, let's go for a walk. ... Will you come with us, Eric?" she asked.

"Sure, just let me finish my coffee."

The handsome threesome set out toward the lake shore and Tuesday had to put her paw into the water.

"I just hope she does not want to go in," Ernestine said with concern in her voice. "It is way too cold for the little thing."

"I am sure she'll find that out very quickly."

Before Eric had finished the sentence, Tuesday had jumped into the clear water and was splashing around. She seemed to have a good time, and both Ernestine and Eric had to laugh at the little creature that was having so much fun.

After a while, Tuesday decided that she'd had enough and swaggered out of the wet. She shook herself and the water droplets sprayed Ernestine and Eric. Eric picked her up and they walked back to the house where Ernestine poured a warm bath for Tuesday. They washed and dried her and before they could say another word, Tuesday was asleep again.

"She is like a baby," said Eric. "She eats, drinks, plays and sleeps. What a life!"

Ernestine looked at him and said mischievously, "Is your life that bad my poor, poor man? I am so sorry for your lot in life."

Eric, surprised by her tone of voice, turned around and looked at her. There was something in her eyes that he had not seen before, a certain glint of humor and almost care-lessness.

"Maybe she is beginning to let go of Jonathan. And maybe soon he will be but a memory and no longer real," he thought to himself. He started to say something but then the phone rang and he answered. His voice lost its carefree tone and became very businesslike. When he had hung up, Ernestine asked, "What was that all about? You sounded so cold and detached?"

"That was the office. I have to leave for South America tomorrow. There is something going on down there that the company wants me to investigate. The cab is already on its way to pick me up. I will meet them at the Dallas office and tomorrow evening fly on to Sao Paulo."

Ernestine was taken aback. She had not realized that she had gotten so used to Eric being around that the prospect of him going away was very unpleasant and disturbing. She followed him upstairs where he had already started to put some clothes into a suitcase.

"How long will you be away?" she asked.

"I really don't know. It depends on what I will find and how it can be fixed."

He did not want her to stand there looking at him with her green eyes full of anxiety. It was almost impossible not to just grab her by her slim waist and pull her towards him and cover her half open, delicious mouth with kisses.

"Could you please check if my blue striped shirt is in the dryer?" he asked her.

Ernestine obediently went downstairs to check for the missing item.

"It is not here," she called, and busied herself in the kitchen.

Ten minutes later, Eric came downstairs with the suitcase packed just as the cab pulled up in the driveway.

"I'll give you a call when I know what's going on," he said, kissed her lightly on the cheek, and was gone.

Ernestine stared after the vanishing cab, then turned and went to look at Tuesday.

"Thank goodness you are here to keep me company." With this thought she went outside to pick a few flowers that were still in the garden and took them into the house.

Chapter 11
A Surprise Visitor

The flight from Portland to Dallas was uneventful and the aircraft touched down on time. The company driver was expecting him at the exit and drove him to the Hilton Hotel. Not being hungry, Eric sat down on the sofa and watched a television show. But he was unable to concentrate on the program, and after a short time he gave up and went to bed.

The next morning, he strolled into the oil company's Dallas office and received his briefing on the troubles in Brazil. He was sent on a fact-finding mission into some discrepancies of oil inventories affecting most companies doing business there. Eric was taken from the offices directly to the airport at Dallas-Fort Worth to catch his flight the same evening.

He checked in, received his boarding pass, went through security, and waited at the Admiral's Club until his flight was being called. Once on the airplane, he thought about the past few weeks and how easy it was to be with Ernestine. He knew that she was the one he wanted to spend the rest of his life with, but he did not know how to tell her that. He was afraid she would push him away and run out on him for good.

During dinner, he mulled the thoughts over in his mind but was far from a solution. After coffee, his mind was still in utter turmoil and he decided to rest for a while. The flight attendants gathered the last pieces of the meal and he put his seat into the sleeping position.

Sleep came quickly, and he was dreaming of Ernestine.

She was dressed in a white, lacy summer gown sitting on the grass, with Tuesday by her side. When she saw him at the edge of the meadow she got up and ran toward him full of joy and happiness with Tuesday at her heel.

She flung herself into his arms and kissed him on his lips. He could feel her breasts pressing against him and his manhood pressing against her leg. Suddenly, he felt a sharp pain in his groin and woke up. The arm rest was pushing against him where he was most vulnerable.

He turned and tried to go back to his dream. Ernestine was still there, but in the kitchen, and she was wearing black tight slacks with a black sweater with silver flowers. Her hair was pulled backwards and she was doing something by the sink. He was unable to see, but when he called out to her she turned around and a sharp butcher's knife was in her hand.

Her eyes were dark and ominous and she came straight at him, arm raised, ready to stab him. But before she was close enough to bring the blade down on him, the flight got bumpy and he woke up sweating.

The flight attendant brought him a glass of water. He drank it in one gulp and went back to sleep. Again, Ernestine was there. This time she was dressed in a teal-gray business suit, a matching starched blouse, black pumps and purse. On her fingers were rings of all types … big ones, small ones, with precious stones and without.

She stood in a room full of boxes and men clad in black stood along those boxes. Eric was facing them with a box on his lap. Ernestine accusingly pointed one bejeweled finger at him and the men started toward him and began to shake him while calling his name.

"Mr. Massy, Mr. Massy, please wake up," the flight attendant said. "You are having a nightmare."

Eric opened his eyes and realized that he was on a plane and not in a room full of boxes with Ernestine and the men in black trying to grab him.

"Bring me some orange juice, please," he asked the flight attendant, and thought about the meaning of these strange and unsettling dreams. Not being able to decipher the meaning, he decided to put it out of his mind for the time being. He needed to have a clear head to deal with whatever emergency was awaiting him at the end of this flight.

He decided to talk to Ernestine on his return and deal with her reaction whatever it may be. With this thought, he fell into a dreamless sleep until the captain's voice came over the intercom that they were going to land shortly at the international airport of Sao Paulo.

Again, he was met by a company driver and brought to the offices in the center of town, where he met with several other engineers that were all brought here to get to the bottom of these problems. They discussed the facts, the existing problems; and opinions and plans were offered on how to best address the issues. Eric was absorbed in his work and had very little time to think about Ernestine.

Meanwhile, back in Oregon, Ernestine spent her days playing with Tuesday. She had even enrolled her in a training class at the local kennel. Twice a week, Ernestine and Tuesday went to the training classes and Tuesday learned very quickly.

At home, they would continue the training; and pretty soon, Ernestine was able to walk with Tuesday at her side without a leash. She would obey Ernestine's commands and the two grew very close.

Ernestine discussed with her the menu of the day, the news, the weather, and her feelings. Tuesday was an excellent listener, never interrupting, looking at her with her big brown dog eyes as if she understood; and sometimes Ernestine felt like Tuesday was going to say something, but she never did.

The days passed by peacefully. There was the occasional phone call from Eric telling her about his progress in some jungle town or other. Soon, the days started to get shorter and shorter and the mornings were chilly. The leaves on the trees began to change color. It was quite a display and Ernestine enjoyed her walks along the lake.

With every day, the colors became more intense; the yellows were golden, the reds like Snow White's lips, the orange like liquid copper. It looked like a painting by Miró with all its intense colors.

On one such day, Ernestine drove into town for grocery shopping and to get Tuesday her last puppy shots. They walked around the village for a while and then headed home.

Arriving at the house, she found a young woman sitting on the front steps. Ernestine parked the car and walked toward her. She was very thin with long shiny black hair; her eyes were slightly slanted and half closed; a thin-lipped mouth gave her a witch-like appearance; and there was something about her that made Ernestine uncomfortable.

When Ernestine was but a few steps from her she got up and asked rather rudely, "Where is Eric?"

"He'll be back in a few days," Ernestine answered, taken aback by the woman's rudeness and obvious dislike for her.

"Are you the cleaning woman?" the thin-lipped one inquired.

"Yes. I stay here while Eric is away and look after the house and his dog."

"Good, then you can arrange a room for me. I will stay until Eric comes back," directed the woman rather snootily.

"Oh, I don't know if Eric would agree to that. I do not even know who you are."

I am Tara. Eric bought the house from my parents a few years ago and, as he was so in love with me, he told me that I was welcome to stay here anytime I wished."

With these words, Tara turned around and motioned to Ernestine to unlock the door and let her in. Ernestine was so stunned by this unfriendly and obnoxious woman and at her own behavior that she silently unlocked the door and let the stranger pass.

"Well," uttered Tara, loud enough for Ernestine to hear, "nothing much has changed in here. Eric could have at least cleaned the place up."

She looked at Ernestine with hatred in her eyes and went upstairs.

"Prepare my room. I want this one," and she opened the door to Ernestine's bedroom. "Don't tell me you are using the best room in the house."

"Yes, this is my room. Eric wanted me to have it," Ernestine replied sharply.

"Don't talk to me like this," Tara barked. "You are only the cleaning woman whereas I am his girlfriend. You can move out right now and I don't care if you sleep in the doghouse."

"No," replied Ernestine softly, "I will not move out. You may have the spare bedroom; and if you don't like it you can leave."

Abruptly, Tara turned around ready to hit Ernestine in the face, but before she knew what had happened, Tara found herself thrown rather unceremoniously on the floor.

"How dare you, you, you…," and she began to sob. Her whole lithe body was shaking; salty tears were running down her cheeks, staining the front of her white silk blouse. When Ernestine extended a hand to help her up, her gray eyes had lost all that snobbishness. She looked more like a hurt animal than the imposing woman she had wanted to portray.

"Come, Tara, let's go downstairs and start over while drinking a cup of tea," said Ernestine, and went down the stairs. Tara followed silently. In the kitchen, Ernestine busied herself making tea and observing Tara from the corner of her eyes. She was wondering whatever had brought Tara here and why she had been trying to be someone she definitely was not. There was a certain shyness and vulnerability about her and some elusive sadness.

"Let's sit down in the living room while the tea is getting ready," suggested Ernestine, and both women walked over to the big bay window and sat down in the soft chairs by the huge fireplace. The silence between them was heavy and Ernestine was glad when the kettle whistled.

She almost jumped out of the chair, eager to get to the kitchen and busy herself with the tea. In a moment, she was back with a tray loaded with two light-blue porcelain cups, the teapot and some cookies she had found in a cupboard. She put the tray on the coffee table and sat down again.

Tara was watching her and finally broke the silence and asked her, "Who are you? I somehow have the feeling that you are not the cleaning woman, am I right?"

"You are right. My husband and Eric were old friends and I have known him for many years. He invited me to stay with him for a while and I accepted. He is away in South America at the moment but he should be back within a week or two at the most. What about you? What brings you here?"

"It is a long story and I do not know where to begin," whispered Tara.

Ernestine was silent and poured the tea. It was some type of black tea that Eric had brought from some of his trips and it was really very aromatic.

"Milk, sugar, or lemon?" asked Ernestine.

"Just black is fine," replied Tara. She took a big sip and began her story.

After her dad had gone bankrupt due to land speculation, their family had moved to Temecula. He had tried his hand at several different things but luck avoided him and they sank deeper and deeper into despair. After a few months, her mother had started divorce proceedings; and when the divorce became final she had moved away leaving fifteen-year-old Tara with her dad. At first, she enjoyed being the only female in her dad's life and getting all his attention.

However, as the weeks passed by, she noticed that her dad happened to be there when she undressed or went to the bathroom.

She had heard enough stories to realize that she was in danger and had to do something. She talked to the principal at school and it was arranged that child protective services would take care of her. She was put into foster care until her dad could prove that nothing had happened and nothing was going to happen, that all this was due to Tara's imagination, girls' talk, and the media's convoluted stories about teenage girls living alone with their dads.

After the courts had decided that it was safe for her to live with her dad she returned to him. Her dad, however, did not forgive her for ruining his reputation and making it impossible for him to get a decent job in this desert town.

They moved north, then east, wherever her dad thought he might find a job. This went on for about a year when one day her mother called and asked Tara to come live with her and her new husband. Tara packed her few things, went to the airport where a ticket was waiting for her, and flew to Los Angeles.

Her mother and her husband were waiting for her and took her to their imposing home in the hills. Gardeners were raking, weeding and planting. Inside, servants were busy dusting, cleaning and putting things in order.

Tara was overwhelmed. She had a huge bedroom suite complete with sitting room and fireplace, a bathroom with Jacuzzi tub, and a shower with several shower heads. It was right out of a movie.

At first, Tara liked the luxury and being pampered, but after a while she got used to it and was looking for something more than just superficialities. Her mother's new lifestyle, she realized, was not hers. She did not want to go to endless boring parties, hearing the same stories over and over again; and one day, she ran away.

She took some of her mother's jewelry and all the money she could find, and made her way to New York. She thought she could be an actress. What disillusion. She ran out of money rather quickly, did not find a job, and had to live together with a bunch of other runaways with big dreams.

When she found out that she was pregnant but did not know who the father was, she decided to quit this life, go back, and try to mend fences with her parents. Her dad was happy to have her back. He had found a job, was working, and had found a pleasant woman whom he had married only a short while before Tara appeared again.

Only Tara did not appreciate being now second in her dad's life and went on a drinking binge. On the way home she had an accident and during the days at the hospital she had lost her unborn child.

"I was discharged a week ago, and not knowing where to go, I thought of Eric," she ended her story.

Ernestine sat silently watching her not quite sure whether the girl was telling the truth or just making up a story to pull on her heartstrings.

"You have had quite some experiences," she finally said. "And I am sorry about your baby."

Both women quietly sat on their sofas watching the sun set in the west, each one of them lost in their own thoughts.

A sudden knock at the front door interrupted their reverie.

"Who could that be?" wondered Ernestine, and walked to the little window to peer at the intruder. But all she saw was a big bouquet of flowers. She opened the door and there stood a man with a huge bouquet of flowers covering his face. But before she could say anything, the flowers were thrust aside and Eric took her in his arms.

"Eric," she whispered, "you are back; how wonderful." Eric did not let her go but kissed her on her soft inviting mouth. He had imagined this moment since his arrival in Sao Paulo when he finally decided to end this agony and ask her to be his wife. He set her free and was about to ask her when he heard a voice say, "Hi Eric."

Eric gasped soundlessly and his face changed from the happy boy's face of a second ago to a mask of impenetrable stone. He had recognized the voice immediately and a flood of unpleasant memories washed over him.

Ernestine, holding the flowers, was watching him in astonishment. Never had she seen him like that. His eyes, radiant with joy a second ago turned ice cold; his mouth, lips pressed together gave his ashen face the look of a plaster statue with all life sapped from him. His eyes did not leave Tara and he icily said, "Tara, what brought you here of all places?"

Before Tara could answer Eric almost shouted, "I don't want to know and I want you out of here now. You know better than showing up here, you little tramp."

With these words, Eric stormed up the stairs and slammed the door to his room. Ernestine stood there with her flowers and looked at Tara who silently had started to cry. Ernestine was confused but more about her own emotions than what she had just witnessed.

When Eric had held her in his arms and gently kissed her, feelings stirred in her that she thought had been buried with Jonathan. That kiss had awakened a yearning she was not prepared to face.

Her thoughts swirled in her head like a maelstrom and she quickly went to the kitchen and put the flowers into a tall crystal vase, took them back to the living room, and went over to Tara. She gently took her by the arm and led her to the sofa where she made her sit down. "Now, Tara, what was all that about? Why did Eric react like this? What has happened here that makes him so angry?"

"It happened many years ago when my dad first lost his job and had proposed to Eric to buy the property at a fire sale price. I was so upset and angry at Eric for accepting my dad's offer that I pretended one morning that Eric had raped me during the night. I figured this would prevent my dad from selling our home to Eric.

However, it was too late to rescind the contract for the sale of the house and we left shortly thereafter. My dad brought charges against Eric but they were finally dropped when I recanted my story. Eric was furious and would not talk to us anymore. I had betrayed him in a most hurting way. I cannot blame him, but I had hoped he would have gotten over it by now. It was just a child's prank."

Ernestine silently listened to her but had the strange feeling that there was more to this story than what Tara had just told her, and that there had been untold consequences of her actions.

She did not believe her either that it was a childish prank. Girls, especially teenage girls, know exactly what they are doing; and Ernestine had the sinking feeling that this was the girl that at one time Eric was in love with and was taken advantage of in a way he could never have anticipated.

Women, including girls, are very calculating and do only those things that will advance their agendas. Anything else is pointless in their eyes and often they do it without thinking about the consequences for themselves or the men they are hurting. They are just wired that way.

Ernestine thought back to the time she first met Jonathan. He was all she ever wanted in a man and decided early on that she wanted to become his wife. All her subsequent actions were aimed at achieving that dream.

"I wasn't any better than Tara," she thought, "only I made my man happy and Tara deeply hurt Eric. Maybe it was her impatience, her immaturity, or something else that made her act that way."

"Ernestine?" Tara whispered, "May I stay tonight? I have nowhere to go."

"I don't think that is a good idea," answered Ernestine. "I'll take you to the hotel in town. Stay here. I'll get your things." With these words Ernestine went upstairs and collected Tara's belongings. She heard Eric in his room and figured it was best to leave him alone and to get Tara away as quickly as possible.

"Let's go Tara," she said brusquely.

They put her things into the trunk of the car and drove off toward the town. Ernestine had her eyes fixed on the road and Tara was staring blindly ahead. At the hotel, Ernestine asked for a room, paid for one night, took Tara to the room, gave her a few hundred-dollar bills and said:

"Here; take this and leave tomorrow morning. Don't come back to the house. Find a place somewhere else and start over."

With these words, Ernestine turned around and left. She did not hear what Tara was shouting. She was not interested enough to hear more. She drove back deep in thoughts and before she realized it she was at the house. Tuesday came out and greeted her passionately as only dogs can do. Absent-mindedly she petted her head and talked to her softly.

When she opened the door, Eric was standing in the kitchen, looking out over the lake with unseeing eyes. Ernestine went to him and told him that she had deposited Tara at the hotel in town. She did not ask him all the questions that were looking for an answer but figured that if he wanted her to know he would tell her in his own good time. She poured herself a cup of freshly-brewed black tea, added some milk, and carried it over to her favorite chair in the den. She sat down and began to leaf through a magazine that was lying on the coffee table.

After a while, Eric joined her and sat down opposite her, watching her looking at the magazine.

"Are you reading?" he asked.

"Nope, I am just looking at the pictures. My mind cannot stay focused long enough for me to do some serious reading," she answered and looked at him.

The stone-like mask had vanished but there was still a somber glimmer in his beautiful eyes that had not been there before tonight and a deep sadness lined his lips. Ernestine wondered if it would ever go away again.

"Want to hear my side of the story?" he asked gloomily.

"When you are ready to tell me, I will listen," she said to him without any judgment in her voice.

"You amaze me. Any other woman would have already pestered me with questions and advice and good intentions. But you, … you are so removed as if you could not care less about me and my past." With these words, Eric got up and angrily went upstairs and slammed his bedroom door for the second time in as many hours.

Ernestine finished her tea, put the dishes into the dishwasher, locked the doors and went upstairs to her own room. She took a bath but it did not bring her the quietness of the soul she was searching for; instead she became more and more agitated. She finally got out of the tepid water, slipped into her pink flannel nightgown and went to bed. Sleep eluded her until early morning when the first rays of the rising sun became visible on the eastern sky.

When she finally awoke, she knew that there was something she had to do, something that had to be clarified. And then she remembered Eric's kiss and the feelings that had arisen in the pit of her stomach. She tried to imagine the kiss and to recreate those feelings, but her mind tricked her and she was kissing Jonathan; and when she came out of her reverie she felt miserable as she had felt after the funeral.

Not only was the pain of Jonathan's loss overwhelming, but she realized that she could no longer stay here. Something had changed; and even though she did not know what it was, her womanly intuition told her that she had to go. She wondered what may have happened had Tara appeared one day later.

With a heavy heart, she started to pack her things, booked a flight to San Diego, and ordered a cab to pick her up. Then she went downstairs and found a note on the kitchen table. Eric had gone for a walk with Tuesday and would be back later. She put the note back on the table, walked around the house where she had been happy, took a last glance at the lake and the meadow and waited for the cab.

It was not long before she heard the black car arrive. She closed the door behind her and knew that another chapter in her life was closed. With tears in her eyes she told the cabbie where to go and looked through the back window of the car until the house disappeared behind the trees.

Chapter 12
Following in Jonathan's Footsteps

Ernestine had been in San Diego for a few weeks when she became restless. She needed something to occupy her. She missed Tuesday and wondered what had become of her and of Eric. She had waited for his phone call but it never came and she decided that she had left in a most inappropriate way.

She realized that she should have stayed and listened to his side of the story instead of fleeing from her own feelings. But it was too late, what is done is done and it could not be undone.

One afternoon, while she was sitting in one of the soft chairs on the balcony reading the paper, a small notice in the back of the paper caught her eyes. St. Vincent de Paul was looking for volunteers to help with serving meals to the homeless.

Ernestine remembered that Jonathan at one time in his life had helped out and that he had been full of praise on how well it was run. He had met the founder, Father Joe Carroll, and was impressed with his insight into human nature. Ernestine grabbed the phone and called the number listed in the paper and was told to come by and fill out an application.

The same afternoon, she strolled over to the center, filled out the required forms, and a week later she helped in the kitchen. It was a huge place, high ceilings, whitewashed walls and red tile floors with several stoves and big shiny pots and pans standing like tin soldiers on the shelves.

The employees and volunteers were friendly and showed her what to do. It was an easy atmosphere and even though she sometimes caught inquisitive eyes following her, nobody ever asked who she was or why she was doing this. They were all happy to have one more pair of hands to help with all the chores. Ernestine most enjoyed serving the meals.

Most guests were friendly, and it was only occasionally that she had to call on the supervisor to have an unruly customer removed. One day, a family of four was sitting at the table she was serving ... the dad, a tall clean-shaven man dressed in a white shirt and tie and impeccably-pressed dress pants; his wife, a cute-looking blonde with the most astonishing blue eyes Ernestine had ever seen; and two little girls with the same hair and eyes as the mother. The four of them sat very still while she was serving them, and before they started to eat they prayed a short thanks-giving prayer.

Ernestine observed the family from a distance and asked the supervisor if he had seen them before. He had not and Ernestine was determined to find out what ill had befallen this little family. After her shift was over, she went to the administrator and asked how she could find out what had happened. However, she was told that they were unable to give her any information.

So Ernestine went home and called Father Carroll directly. She introduced herself as Jonathan's wife and stated her business. Father Carroll invited her over to his office where she explained the reasons for wanting to know more about that family.

"I can arrange for you to meet with them if they consent to do so," Father Carroll answered her request. "We are unable to give out information about any of our guests for obvious reasons."

"Please make the arrangements and let me know," Ernestine replied, got up and left.

Father Carroll sat quietly for a moment and wondered what had triggered the woman's interest in this particular family.

When Ernestine got home, a visitor was waiting for her.

"Mary-Ann," she exclaimed, "so good to see you!"

"Likewise," Mary-Ann smiled. "It's been a while since we had a good talk. Do you have time now or are you busy?"

"No, no, please come; we shall talk like we used to."

The two elegant women entered the elevator that brought them to Ernestine's floor.

"Come in and have a seat while I get out of these clothes," said Ernestine.

A few minutes later she was back in faded jeans, an oversized sea-green sweater, and her hair pulled to a pony tail.

"You seem happy enough," mused Mary-Ann. "What are you up to?"

"I've just been to see Father Carroll from the St. Vincent de Paul center and he'll help me get some information about a family that is staying there. They seemed to have fallen on hard times, not at all your regular homeless people, and I want to see if I can help them somehow."

"That is very generous of you."

"Well you see, I never thought of it; but the little voice in my head was whispering in my ear and I chose to follow that. I will let you know what is going to happen. And what about you? How are you coping?"

Mary-Ann looked at Ernestine and started to tell her what it has been like the past few months while Ernestine was in Oregon. Things between Kevin and her had not improved. On the contrary, things had gotten worse and worse and Mary-Ann was contemplating a divorce.

At first, Kevin was okay with the special sexual arrangements for Mary-Ann but a few weeks ago he became verbally abusive when she came home after one of these encounters. He had also started drinking and abusing drugs again.

"I am afraid that one day he'll beat me up or worse," Mary-Ann said. "I cannot go on in this way and I have pretty much made up my mind to leave him but I don't know how to tell him. He is so vulnerable, but he also wallows in self-pity which I cannot stand."

"Oh Mary-Ann, I am so sorry," replied Ernestine. "I had no idea. But why don't you come and live with me until you have sorted out the details of your dilemma and your divorce? I have enough room here and the separation may be good for the both of you."

"Thanks for the offer. Let me think about it and I will let you know."

The women were silent for a long while, each one of them following their own train of thoughts. Mary-Ann thought about the effects on Kevin should she leave, and Ernestine was wondering what Eric and Tuesday were up to.

The sun started to set and Mary-Ann got up, took her tall glass to the kitchen and bid Ernestine a good evening. Ernestine locked the door behind her when the phone started to ring. It was Father Carroll who told her that the family would be pleased to meet her at her convenience.

They arranged to meet the next day at the Pier Café at Seaport Village. Father Carroll would pick them up and bring them over. Ernestine was happy to meet them but at the same time she wasn't quite sure what she had in mind. She figured that her little voice would be there and guide her. After she had cleaned up her kitchen she went to bed and was asleep as soon as her head rested on the soft pillow.

At eight o'clock, her alarm clock rang and she jumped out of bed. She felt great, as if a heavy burden had been lifted from her shoulders. She stepped into the shower and let the warm water run down her slim body. She shampooed her hair, and suddenly she felt an unbearable urge between her legs that she had only felt when Jonathan was with her. She gently touched herself and almost immediately her body reacted. Intense relief washed over her as all the pent-up emotions were released. She stood under the shower shuddering; and when it was over, she started to cry. She dried herself with Jonathan's big fluffy towel and tried to think happy thoughts, but her tears kept on coming. She put her panties and bra on and went to the kitchen to pour some orange juice.

"Get a grip on yourself," she admonished herself.

And slowly, her tears stopped flowing, her heart beat steadily again, and her mood improved. She walked into her closet and carefully chose a pair of dark-blue jeans, a blue-and-white-striped t-shirt, and a yellow cardigan. She pulled her hair into a pony tail and slipped into her favorite Italian sandals. She snatched her little purse from the hall table, took the elevator to the lobby, and walked out into the sunshine. Seaport Village was only a couple of blocks away and Ernestine enjoyed the short walk.

When she approached the Pier Café she saw Father Carroll with his charges arriving from the opposite side. She waved, and all of them were quickly seated by a window with a view of Coronado. Father Carroll introduced the family as Mr. and Mrs. Connor with their daughters Emily and Ashley.

After Mr. Connor had lost his job, they were unable to make their mortgage payments, and about a week ago the bank foreclosed on their home. They were left with nothing as they had sold off everything of value, even the wife's car, in order to save their home.

"Emily, Ashley, would you like to ride the merry-go-round?" asked Father Carroll. The eyes of both girls lit up and they looked pleadingly at their dad.

"By all means, go and enjoy the ride," he said.

And off they went. Ernestine wanted to know where they had lived and what job he was looking for. They had lived in Las Vegas and he had worked as an accountant for a small aviation company that went under.

After they were kicked out of their home, they came to San Diego, hoping to stay with some family. But upon their arrival they found that some other relatives were already living there and there was no room for them. Unable to afford a hotel they ended up at St. Vincent de Paul.

"Yesterday was our first day there," whispered the woman.

"I have an idea," said Ernestine. "I own a furnished rental that is vacant at the moment, and you can stay there. Then I will see what we can do about a job for you."

"Why are you doing this?" asked Mr. Connor.

"I don't really know, but it is something I have to do. My husband would have done the same thing and I'd like to think that he'd have approved."

Ernestine left it at that and called her property manager to arrange for the Connors to move immediately into the house. Then she called Kevin and a few friends of Jonathan and explained the situation. They promised to look out for anything that might come up for Mr. Connor.

Ernestine paid the waitress and led Mr. and Mrs. Connor to the merry-go-round where Father Carroll was watching the girls.

"All set?" he inquired.

"Yes," said Ernestine. "We'll go back to the shelter, pick up their belongings, and I will take them to their new lodging. You are very welcome to come along, Father."

The girls jumped off their horses and came running to their parents. Their eyes shone with pleasure but they became still as they saw their mom silently crying. Father Carroll took them by the hand and told them that they were going to move to another place.

The little group vanished into Father Carroll's car and Ernestine quickly walked home to pick up her car and meet them at the shelter. No sooner had she arrived there than the Connors were ready to leave. The girls went with Father Carroll and Mr. and Mrs. Connor went with Ernestine.

"We cannot thank you enough, Mrs. Leclerc," they said and remained silent for the rest of the trip.

After a short time, they arrived at a little bungalow in Normal Heights.

"Here we are!" exclaimed Ernestine. She stopped her car and got out. The Connors followed her. The property manager was already there and had opened the door. It was a small house with yellow siding, red brick roof and a white front porch. The windows were framed with little white curtains and a few steps led to the entrance.

The property manager had opened the windows and a gentle breeze came in, dispersing the musky smell of a house that has been left vacant for a while. The rooms were small and a few pieces of furniture had been left behind by the last tenant. They were in good shape and the Connors were happy to have them. The girls arrived and stormed into the house. They were happy and were wondering if they could have a little dog in the back yard.

"Where is your car?" asked Ernestine, and was told that they had to leave it behind at the shelter as they had run out of gas and had no money to fill the tank.

"As soon as I get paid at whatever job I may find, I will get the car. I can leave it there until then," Mr. Connor answered.

"Let's get it now; you might need it sooner than you think. How will you get around this town without a vehicle? Public transportation is not exactly blooming here." Ernestine smiled and went to her car with Mr. Connor in tow.

A short while later, they were back with the Connor's car, and he parked it in the driveway. This time, his eyes were moist as he thanked Ernestine.

"There is a small supermarket around the corner so you can get the necessary things for tonight. Make a list of items you will need and I will be back tomorrow morning. Have a good evening." With these words, Ernestine gave Mrs. Connor an envelope and went to her car and drove off.

Mrs. Connor opened the envelope and found several hundred dollar bills and a few smaller ones. Silently she showed the money to her husband and both of them watched that red-haired elegant woman drive away.

"She must be an angel or something like that," whispered Mrs. Connor. "Who else would help a stranger?"

"I have no answer for you, my dear," answered her husband in a low voice. "Maybe there is a God after all watching over us."

They softly closed the front door and walked hand in hand through the house, watching the girls play in the back yard.

Back at her condo, Ernestine kicked off her shoes, went to the fridge and poured herself a glass of lemonade. She took it to the balcony and sat down in Jonathan's chair. There were a few clouds in the sky and the sun was setting. A large, white seagull landed on the bronze railing. Ernestine watched intensely as the bird started to clean itself and, after what seemed a long time, took flight again. Ernestine's eyes followed the seagull until it vanished over the water.

"I wonder where it is going and what brought it here in the first place?" mused Ernestine; but before she could find any answers, the phone started to ring. It was Father Carroll who wanted to know how the Connors were doing. They talked for a while and Ernestine assured him that she would look after them until they were on their feet again.

"If I have any problems I will call you, Father. Have a good evening, and thanks for letting me do this," she said.

"You truly are Jonathan's wife in every respect," he said. "He would have done exactly the same. God bless you, Ernestine."

After a good night's sleep, Ernestine went back to the Connor's place to see what else was needed to give them a good new start. She found the family sitting at the kitchen table enjoying breakfast. They made room for her and, while drinking a cup of coffee, they decided what needed to be done first.

"The girls need to be enrolled in school," said Mrs. Connor, "and after that there are a few items that we need. Maybe there are some second-hand stores around where we can find some of these things."

"I'll ask my property manager who lives nearby. I am sure she'll know," answered Ernestine. She called the woman who had taken care of Jonathan's rentals for him for years and she agreed to come over and go with the Connors to several places. When she arrived, Ernestine got up, said good-bye to the Connors and drove home.

Chapter 13
Mary-Ann's Sorrow

She spent the next few days reading, watching television, and going for long walks along the bay. Sometimes she thought of Eric and Tara and wondered what had become of them.

The one she really missed was Tuesday but she knew that the dog was better off with Eric than cooped up in the condo with her. She was contemplating getting a small dog that would not mind being indoors most of the time and that would make a great companion for her.

One day, returning from her walk, the phone was ringing and an unknown voice asked, "Is this Mrs. Leclerc?"

"It is she," Ernestine answered. "Who wants to know?"

"This is Captain Richard, San Diego Police. Do you know a Mrs. Mary-Ann Masters?"

"Yes I do, Officer. What has happened?"

"Do you mind coming over to her place now? I'll have an officer pick you up in a few minutes."

"Of course; but why?"

"We'll talk when you get here. Thanks Mrs. Leclerc," the voice said and he hung up the phone.

Ernestine stood there with the phone in her hands while a million thoughts raced through her mind like a swarm of killer bees after a victim.

Before she had time to put on her shoes, the doorbell rang and a police officer flashed his badge in front of her eyes and motioned her to come with him.

Silently, they drove in the police cruiser to Mary-Ann's house. There were a lot of cars parked all over the street and Ernestine could make out several media vans from all the networks due to their shouting logos.

"What is going on here?" she shouted at the police driver who maneuvered the cruiser around loud reporters, curious bystanders, and other people that had nothing better to do on a beautiful San Diego day.

"We'll be there in a minute, and the captain will explain," replied the young officer.

At the house, Ernestine got out and, accompanied by the driver, was led into the living room where she saw Mary-Ann sitting on the sofa surrounded by police officers in uniform, and detectives busy with their gadgets trying to retrieve fingerprints from tables, furniture, doors and anything that was in sight.

Before she could say anything, she was led into the kitchen where the police captain was talking on the phone. When he saw her he turned around and offered her a seat.

"I am sorry Mrs. Leclerc, but Mr. Masters was stabbed to death early this morning. Everything points to his wife as the perpetrator."

Ernestine was dumbfounded.

"Kevin dead? Mary-Ann accused of killing him? Why? I have to talk to Mary-Ann."

She almost overturned the chair and slammed into a tall officer who entered the kitchen.

"I'm sorry," she stammered and crossed the living room to embrace her friend who was sitting there like a statue, motionless, her kind face distorted in agony, and her hands clenching and unclenching incessantly.

Ernestine put her arms around her friend and looked deep into those big dark eyes glittering with raw hurt. A war of emotions raged within her as she tried to control herself. Instinctively, Ernestine understood that now was not the time to ask questions.

So she sat there beside her troubled friend holding her, trying to be the rock that Mary-Ann had always been when she needed her. Ernestine had lost track of how long they had been sitting there, both lost in their own thoughts.

One by one, the police officers and detectives left the house until only the captain remained. He came over to the two women and pulled a chair to the coffee table and sat down opposite them.

"I have to ask you to tell me again how this happened, Mrs. Masters," he said with his deep resonating voice.

Mary-Ann looked up at him and hesitantly started to speak, her voice hardly audible. "I had come home from work at around 4:00 am and went to the kitchen to make myself a sandwich. All of a sudden I heard my husband coming down the stairs screaming about something I could not make out.

He stormed into the kitchen, grabbed a knife and came at me. Before I knew what happened, he was on the ground, bleeding profusely, and I was standing there, holding a bloody butcher's knife. I tried to stem the bleeding and then called 911."

"Did you have any marital problems?" the captain asked.

Mary-Ann glanced at Ernestine and answered truthfully, "In a way, yes." She briefly told the officer of the arrangement she and her husband had and that this had been going on since his boating accident a few years ago.

"Was your husband complaining about any pains?"

"He has become more irritable lately, but he did not complain about pain," Mary-Ann said sadly.

The officer said, "Mrs. Masters, I have to ask you not to leave town until this case is closed."

With these words he got up and left. Ernestine caught up with him and asked what was going to happen next. "There will be an investigation and, depending on the outcome, your friend will either go free or to jail." With these harsh words he turned and marched to his car.

"I killed Kevin, I stabbed him to death. Oh Ernestine, I did not mean it. He just came at me with the knife swinging over his head. I don't really know what happened. Where did I get the butcher's knife from? Was it on the counter or in the drawer? I just can't remember. It all happened so quickly. Oh my god, Kevin is dead, really dead? He will never speak to me again. I will never hear his voice again. Touch his beloved face. I so love him, Ernestine. What am I going to do?"

"I'll stay here with you, or you come and stay with me at my place," Ernestine said. "I will figure out what needs to be done."

Ernestine left Mary-Ann on the sofa and went to the phone in the hallway. She could not bear going into the kitchen where Kevin's body had lain. Blood was still on the floor and she needed to get someone to clean up the mess.

Her first call went to Kevin's office where she talked to an associate of his and left a message for his boss to call back. She then called the cleaning service, the funeral parlor, family and close friends.

The call to Kevin's family was harrowing. His mother answered the call thinking it was Kevin. When she was told, she started sobbing uncontrollably. Finally a male voice, Kevin's dad, asked, "Who is this?"

Ernestine identified herself and told the man what she had just told his wife. There was a moment's silence on the other end of the phone line and then the harsh voice was back yelling, "We'll be there as soon as possible," and he hung up.

Ernestine stared at the receiver and thought how different people react to sad news. She then went back to the living room where Mary-Ann still sat in the same position Ernestine had left her. Her heart was aching for her friend and she wished there was something she could do to alleviate the pain. But she knew from her own experience that only time could help Mary-Ann.

An old saying her grandmother often used came to her mind:

Time will heal
Time will mend
Do not break
But bend!

She remembered that a long time ago, when she stayed with her grandparents for those long summer vacations, her grandmother had taken her to a funeral in the village. Ernestine did not quite understand what was going on but she felt the pain and sorrow of the people around her. Her grandmother had then said to her:

"Always remember, my little one, that only time can help those in pain."

Looking at her friend, she realized that she had to get Mary-Ann to bed. The color had drained from her face and it was white as a sheet. Her beautiful eyes were without expression; and her whole lithe body was slumped against the back of the sofa.

Before Ernestine could say anything, the doorbell rang. Mary-Ann did not even hear it, so Ernestine went to open the door. Kevin's partner and friend Tom, together with another man whom Ernestine did not recognize, stood there. Both had sad faces.

"Hi, Ernestine," said Tom, "this is Durban our doctor in the building. I thought I'd bring him along to look after Mary-Ann."

"Very thoughtful of you," replied Ernestine. She had never liked Tom but now was surprised at his thoughtfulness.

"Please come in. I was just about to take Ernestine to her room and I am really glad Durban that you are here."

"Not a problem," he replied in a soft voice that put Ernestine instantly at ease.

They all went to the living room where Mary-Ann still remained in the same position. Durban went to her and tenderly took her by her arm and lifted her off the sofa and guided her toward the stairs saying, "Ernestine and I will put you to bed. You need to sleep and rest."

He motioned to Ernestine to precede them up the stairs to Mary-Ann's bedroom. While he prepared a sedative for Mary-Ann, Ernestine undressed her and put her to bed. She closed the thick curtains and a peaceful light enveloped the room.

The doctor gave Mary-Ann the sedative; and both he and Ernestine left the room, gently closing the door behind them. Silently, they went downstairs where more friends had arrived. Some had brought finger foods, others flowers or soft drinks. Ernestine went to the kitchen and busied herself with plates and glasses. She knew many of the people and some faces were unfamiliar to her. She moved among them without really noticing anyone in particular until a deep baritone voice said, "Hi, Ernestine."

She spun around and looked into eyes dark as the ocean on a stormy day. She was staring at Eric.

"Eric," she gasped "where are you coming from?"

"I was in the neighborhood when I got a phone call from a friend who told me about Kevin. I thought I'd pass by and see if I can be of any help to Mary-Ann or you," he added.

Ernestine was about to ask about Tara but realized just in time that this was neither the place nor the time to bring up those painful memories.

Instead she said:

"At the moment we are alright. As soon as Mary-Ann is able I'll take her to my apartment to be away from here; and when all of this is over we might go away for a bit. But I have to talk to Mary-Ann first. All the same, thanks for offering your help."

With these words, Ernestine turned her back to Eric and moved away through the crowd. As evening approached, more and more people crammed the living room and kitchen and Ernestine was busy trying to remember names and relationships.

Finally, Kevin's parents arrived and Ernestine was glad that Tom took care of them. The three of them sat in a corner and Tom told them the little that was known at this time. From time to time they glanced at Ernestine who was clearing away dirty dishes, glasses, and cutlery. She piled everything neatly into the new dishwasher and turned it on. Just then, Tom called to her, "Ernestine, please come for a moment."

And she went into the living room and sat down beside Tom.

"Is it true that Mary-Ann stabbed our son?" asked Kevin's dad.

"As far as I know that is true, but we do not yet know exactly why. Kevin seemingly came rushing down the stairs swinging a knife intent on killing Mary-Ann. She grabbed something and when she came to, Kevin was lying on the floor, bleeding profusely. She tried to stem the blood flow, but it was too late. She called 911, and the police were here all morning. We should know more in a few days, after the autopsy," replied Ernestine.

She could feel the hatred of this man in the room as if it was palpable and she quickly said, "If you need me, I am upstairs."

"We are staying at the hotel around the corner and we'll be back tomorrow morning." With these words, Kevin's parents stormed out of the house.

"They do not much like Mary-Ann, do they?" said Tom.

"No, they never have," answered Ernestine.

"You know why?"

"I don't really know, but it has always been that way."

"Well," Tom said, "I shall be going," and handed Ernestine his business card. "Call me anytime if you girls need anything at all."

"Thanks."

What a day, thought Ernestine. It seemed to be never-ending. She quietly went upstairs and looked in on Mary-Ann. Seeing that her friend was sound asleep, she decided to stay overnight in the spare bedroom. She found some sheets and made herself a bed. Sleep overcame her quickly and she slept a dreamless sleep.

Only too quickly morning came and with it all the memories of yesterday. Ernestine jumped out of bed and looked in on Mary-Ann. She was tossing and turning and about to wake up. Ernestine stood in the door frame watching, not sure what to do. Unwanted thoughts filled her mind as she watched Mary-Ann. She quietly turned when a small voice called out to her:

"Ernestine? Please don't go; sit here with me."

Slowly, Ernestine turned and moved toward the bed. Mary-Ann stared at her with glazed eyes and asked:

"Kevin is dead, isn't he? I killed him, didn't I? Oh, Ernestine, I don't quite remember what happened. Help me, please?"

"You called 911 after you tried stopping the blood from leaving his body. The police found you sitting beside him with a bloody knife in your hand and a knife in his hand. They took fingerprints and whatever they thought would be useful to their investigation. The police captain will probably come around again today to ask more questions."

"Where is Kevin's body?"

"It was taken to the county morgue. An autopsy will be performed that may shed some light on this whole affair."

"Oh Ernestine, what am I going to do?"

"I don't know Mary-Ann, but we'll figure something out. Tom was here yesterday, and despite the fact that I don't quite like him he is a great help. He is organizing the funeral and all that goes with it."

Just as Mary-Ann wanted to say something the doorbell rang and Ernestine went to open the door. The police captain stood there with another officer.

"Please come in," Ernestine said and stepped aside to let them pass.

"Is Mrs. Masters awake?"

"Yes, I'll tell her that you are here."

"I am here," she said, coming down the stairs.

"Good morning, Mrs. Masters," said the captain gently. "I have some disturbing news for you."

Mary-Ann looked at him with eyes wide open but not quite taking in what the captain was saying.

"An autopsy was performed on your husband last night and it showed that he had a brain tumor in advanced stadium. Were you aware of this?"

"A brain tumor? Kevin? That is impossible. Are you quite sure?" she asked.

"I have the report here, see for yourself." With these words he handed her the manila folder and Mary-Ann started to read. Her hands started to shake and her body became very still.

"I see," she said. "The brain tumor caused his headaches and his altered personality. He just never said how bad the headaches really were. And I, I never asked him. This explains his terrible mood swings that I thought were due to our strained relationship."

Mary-Ann fell silent as an acute sense of loss filled her whole being while grief and despair tore at her heart.

The captain was observing her and finally broke the silence by saying, "Please come with me to the police station. We have to deal with some formalities before the body can be released to you, or to someone designated by you, for the funeral."

"I will drive her downtown," offered Ernestine, "if that is okay with you."

"Fine; we'll see you there around 11 am. Just ask for Captain Reynolds," and he turned and left the house.

Mary-Ann took a quick shower, donned a charcoal business suit over a Wedgwood blue chiffon blouse, and slipped into a pair of low-heeled black pumps. She twirled her dark hair into a bun and both women left together for the police station.

Captain Reynolds was awaiting them in his spacious office and offered them a seat. He had the papers ready for Mary-Ann's signature.

"There will be no further investigation and you are free to take his body for the funeral."

Mary-Ann signed without reading the papers the captain put before her. When all was done, the two women left and Ernestine called Tom to have him deal with the body.

"Let's go to my apartment," suggested Ernestine, but Mary-Ann was adamant about going to her own place.

"There will be people coming and I have to sort his things, especially his papers; and then there is his family to deal with. Please come with me, Ernestine," pleaded Mary-Ann.

"Of course I'll come with you."

When they arrived at the house, Kevin's family was impatiently waiting and demanded to know where Mary-Ann had gone.

"Please Ernestine, deal with them. I cannot stomach the lot right now," and with these words she entered the hallway and went upstairs, closing the bedroom door with a bang.

Ernestine was just about to explain where they had spent the past hours when she spotted Tom in his red sports car driving up to the house. She waived at him and he quickly came to her aid. He greeted everyone with a grave face and invited them inside. Once everyone was seated he began to speak in his low steady voice:

"Mary-Ann was at the downtown police station taking care of formalities needed to have Kevin's body released. It has been taken to the funeral parlor where it will be cremated tomorrow afternoon according to his wishes. There will be a brief ceremony at the funeral home. Everyone is invited to join us there at 2:00 pm tomorrow afternoon. Here is my business card with directions to the funeral home. If you have any questions, you may call me anytime. And now, I think it best if you go back to your hotel and we meet again tomorrow afternoon."

Kevin's family was stunned but followed Tom's instructions and all of them left.

"Thanks Tom, I could never have pulled this off. They are overpowering."

"Well, they just lost their son and brother so it is understandable."

"Is everything arranged then for the funeral?"

"Yes, it will be a short ceremony according to Kevin's wishes. You know, reading his will, I got the feeling that he knew that time was short for him. At least he left Mary-Ann well provided for, but his family will not see a dime, and I think that might cause even further animosity between them and Mary-Ann."

"She was never close to any of them and I think that even Kevin was not that close either."

"Do you or Mary-Ann need anything else right now?"

"No, we are fine. And thanks again for coming by at the right moment."

"I'll stop by tonight to fill you both in on tomorrow's happenings."

Tom turned and left quickly. Ernestine looked after him and thought, "I might have been mistaken about his personality and maybe I was wrong to dislike him."

She slowly turned and entered the house. She went to the kitchen and got herself an ice-cold coke from the fridge.

She slowly poured it into a tall glass and sipped the dark liquid pensively.

Her thoughts went to Jonathan's funeral. It had been a rare rainy day and she tried to remember the sequence of events, but to no avail. Her memory seemed to have blocked out that day completely. Ernestine sighed and wished she could spare her friend tomorrow's grueling happenings.

She took her glass to the living room and sat down on one of the soft chairs, stretching her long legs and taking a magazine that was lying on the coffee table. She tried to read but her thoughts were unable to concentrate on the letters. Her heart ached and she felt so helpless.

"What would Jonathan do right now?" she wondered. His image appeared in front of her mind's eye and that comforted her. She got up and said to herself, "I will not dwell on what was but I shall go to the kitchen and fix something to eat for Mary-Ann and myself." Action followed the thought. Ernestine rummaged through the fridge and prepared some delicious little sandwiches, whole wheat bread with some lettuce, tomatoes, red onions, salami, and some mascarpone to top it off. She was just about done when she heard Mary-Ann coming down the stairs.

"In the kitchen," she called out and Mary-Ann appeared in the doorway. She looked drawn and her beautiful dark eyes resembled dark ponds on a dark and cloudy day.

"I made us some sandwiches."

"Thanks, but I am not hungry," said Mary-Ann. "I think I'll go upstairs again and lay down."

"Please, have a bite to eat. After that we will call it a day and go to bed."

Listlessly, Mary-Ann sat down and started to munch on one of the tasty little sandwiches.

"Did his family show up?" she asked.

"Yes, they came and Tom told them that you were at the police station and to meet us tomorrow afternoon at the funeral home."

"And they left?"

"Yes, he was very professional and did not give them any alternative."

"Good."

They ate the rest of the sandwiches in silence, each one absorbed in their own thoughts.

"Good night, Ernestine, and thanks for everything. I shall see you tomorrow morning."

With these words, Mary-Ann got up and climbed the stairs to her bedroom where she softly closed the door.

Ernestine cleaned up, closed the doors and windows, and followed her friend to the upper floor. She briefly listened at Mary-Ann's door but there was only silence. So she quietly went to her room and, after reading for a little while, fell asleep.

The next morning when she awoke, the sun was already high in the sky. Alarmed, she looked at the clock and to her dismay saw that it was already 10:00 am. She jumped out of bed, took a quick shower, and ran down the stairs. Mary-Ann was already up and had made coffee.

"You sleep well?" Ernestine asked.

"Yes, I took some sleeping pills to help me relax."

Ernestine put her arm around Mary-Ann's shoulder and said, "It will pass like everything, and time will heal the wounds, or at least make them less painful."

"I know. It's just that I wish this day would already be over. I don't even know how to get to the funeral parlor."

"Don't worry. Tom will pick us up in plenty of time and drive us to the funeral home. There he and I will stand with you to greet the visitors and receive their condolences. It will be alright."

Ernestine looked at her friend and smiled encourage-ingly. She could see that Mary-Ann was fighting some battle within herself but understood that she was not to pry. Once Mary-Ann was ready, she'd tell her; and if not, it was none of her business.

She went toward the kitchen when the doorbell rang. It was Tom.

"Good that you are here," she said. "Want a cup of coffee?"

"Sure, thanks."

Slowly he walked toward Mary-Ann and held her while talking to her in a low voice. Ernestine could not hear what he was saying but it made Mary-Ann's face light up. He must have seen Ernestine's questioning look and said, "I just told her that I found Kevin's relatives outside the house and told them to go to the funeral parlor as the wake would be held there and that there was nothing for them here."

"Thanks Tom," said Ernestine, and felt a little twinge of unease seeing him being so familiar with Mary-Ann.

Both Mary-Ann and Ernestine went upstairs to change for the funeral. They both wore black and both looked stunning. Ernestine with her red hair loosely swept up into a bun and Mary-Ann her dark hair pulled back tightly and held in place with a silver hair comb. Neither of them wore any jewelry except their wedding bands. Their make-up was soft and flattering. The only difference were the shoes, Mary-Ann wore pumps and Ernestine high-heeled dress shoes.

"I wish I was going out with these two ladies rather than going to the funeral of Mary-Ann's husband," thought Tom. He offered them his arms and they walked to his car parked at the curb.

They silently drove to the funeral home where Tom took charge and placed Mary-Ann and Ernestine at the entrance to the little room where Kevin was resting in his coffin. Mary-Ann gasped as she saw him but Ernestine pressed her hand and whispered, "It will pass, Mary-Ann, it will pass."

Kevin's family was among the first to enter the little parlor and unsmilingly greeted Mary-Ann. Friends and colleagues followed and the three greeted all of them.

Finally, it was time to sit down and the pastor addressed the congregation. He talked about life and death, God's will and forbearance, and recited a brief history of Kevin's life and achievements. Before Ernestine realized it, the service was over and she, Mary-Ann and Tom were once again shaking sweaty hands.

At last, the parlor was empty and the coffin taken to the crematorium. Later in the week, the urn with the ashes would be delivered to Mary-Ann.

Tom took the two women back but did not stay. He reminded them to be at the attorney's office next day at 10:00 am for the reading of the will. They acknowledged it and went inside.

"Hungry?" asked Ernestine.

"No, I just want to lie down and forget for a while," replied Mary-Ann.

They embraced and went upstairs to their bedrooms. Even though it was still early, Ernestine was exhausted. Not so much physically but psychologically. She remembered more and more from Jonathan's funeral and she did not want to deal with it right now. She took a little purple pill, crawled under the duvet and went to sleep.

Next morning, Mary-Ann's voice woke her up: "Ernestine, it is 9:00 am and we should get ready to go to the attorney's office."

"Thanks for waking me up. I will be downstairs in a few minutes." Ernestine quickly showered and donned a dark blue business suit and matching pumps. She tied her hair at the back of her head and ran downstairs.

"I am ready," she called to Mary-Ann.

"Good, let's go."

Ernestine drove them to the downtown law office and they both were shown into a spacious wood-paneled office. Tall bookcases lined two walls, and from the huge window one could see the San Diego harbor. Kevin's family was already seated and they looked like vultures ready for the kill. Ernestine thought, "It is better not to have family than these people."

When everyone was seated, the portly attorney at the head of the heavy table opened his file and began to read. Ernestine looked out the window and remembered how often she and Jonathan had sailed through the bay on their way to the open sea. Her reverie was interrupted by a sudden commotion. The relatives were just told that all of Kevin's estate was going to Mary-Ann as his wife and love of his life. They shouted angry words at Mary-Ann and left the office in a disorderly manner. Mary-Ann just sat there and stared out the window.

"Is it over now?" she asked.

"Yes," said Tom and took her by the arm. "Just sign here and you can go home."

She signed on the dotted line, thanked the attorney, and walked together with Ernestine and Tom to the car.

"Is this how a man's life is measured? By how much money he is going to leave to everyone?"

Tom and Ernestine were silent. Mary-Ann got into the car; Ernestine thanked Tom, followed Mary-Ann into the car, and drove to the house.

Next morning when Mary-Ann came downstairs, she found Ernestine pouring over some travel magazines.

"I had brilliant idea," said Ernestine. "We will go away for a while. I have booked tickets and a hotel and I will also pack for you. All you have to do is get dressed and ready to go to the airport. The flight leaves in three hours."

Mary-Ann looked at her and said, "I can't. I have to go to work."

"Right, you'd make a great doctor right now, with your thoughts anywhere but on your patient. And anyway, I called the hospital and told them that you were going to be away for at least a month. They thought it was an excellent idea. So you have no choice but to come with me."

"Where are we going?" asked Mary-Ann.

"It is a surprise but I know you will approve."

Chapter 14
Some Distance

The flight was uneventful and both were happy when the plane landed. Once at the gate they deplaned and called a cab. The driver took their luggage and piled it into the boot of his cab.

"How did you know to take me to Puerto Rico?" asked Mary-Ann, her hair blowing around her pale face.

"It is where you took me after Jonathan's accident and I remembered how healing it was to watch the smooth waves for hours, just sitting in the warm sun, thinking of nothing at all."

They arrived quickly at the hotel, checked in and were taken to their rooms.

"Let's meet at the lobby in an hour," Ernestine said, and Mary-Ann nodded her agreement.

When they met at the lobby an hour later, both had changed from their travel clothes into light pants and t-shirts. They looked like two sisters on a crusade. They sat down on the soft upholstered chairs and ordered a drink.

"I have rented a villa by the sea for the two of us in the west of the island," said Ernestine. "I thought it might be more relaxing than staying in a hotel, and I could not bring myself to stay at the same hotel we stayed at last time we were in Puerto Rico."

"I understand," said Mary-Ann, "and I am quite happy to turn into a housewife for a while. It will keep my mind away from Kevin, at least during the day."

"We will rent a car and drive there tomorrow morning and like this we will be able to move around easily."

Their drinks arrived and they sipped the ice cold beverages silently. Both women were deep in thought. Both thinking of their husbands and how life had brought them together. They decided to skip dinner and have an early night.

Next morning, the car was brought around and they left for Rincon. It was a long and painful drive out of San Juan, but once they hit the open road traffic eased and they enjoyed the lush scenery. They drove through green hills dotted with houses, along the coast overlooking the ocean, and on winding little roads until they finally arrived at their destination.

Ernestine had rented a villa next to a small resort. It was right by the sandy beach; only a few steps from the door was the water inviting them for a swim. The bedrooms were spacious and furnished in a rustic style with soft white beds and black marble bathrooms with gold-plated fixtures. The kitchen was fully furnished, and even the fridge had been stocked with necessary items. A little map on the kitchen island showed them where to find stores and restaurants. The women carried their luggage to their rooms and unpacked.

"I am done," called Mary-Ann from the hallway.

"So am I," replied Ernestine. "Let's go for a swim."

They ran down the few steps to the beach and dived into the inviting blue water of the Caribbean. They splashed around for a while and finally walked out of the water, dripping from head to toe, looking like two wet poodles.

"I need a shower," laughed Ernestine and grabbed Mary-Ann's hand, "and then let's go to town and find a grocery store."

"Sounds good to me," replied Mary-Ann.

They showered and then went exploring the little town. There was not much to do but they found a grocery store where they bought some fruit and vegetables. At a nearby place they bought some sandwiches for the evening. When they returned to the villa, they found a huge basket of flowers on the doorstep. It was addressed to Mary-Ann and a little card peeked out from between the flowers. When

Mary-Ann read the card, her eyes twinkled and became luminous.

"They are from Tom. How did he know where we were going to be?"

"He insisted I tell him, so I did," said Ernestine.

Mary-Ann fell silent and took the flowers inside and put them on the coffee table by the big picture window. Then she helped Ernestine carry the groceries to the kitchen. They put the fruit in a bowl on the kitchen island and the veggies in the fridge. They arranged their sandwiches on little yellow plates and carried them to the two big mauve chairs that were facing the water. Ernestine brought some Coke and they sat silently munching on their sandwiches. After a while Mary-Ann broke the silence saying:

"I know you are wondering why Tom would send me flowers and I will tell you. Many years ago, we met at a Christmas party at Kevin's office and we realized that we knew one another from way back in Indiana.

He attended the same high school I did but we were never close. To him, and many of his friends, I was an oddity, an Amish girl in a public high school; so they left me alone for the most part.

He was impressed with my career and thought it great that I had insisted on pursuing my dream. Thereafter, he came a few times to the house for parties and so on. When the accident with Kevin happened he was there to support us not knowing exactly what the consequences of the accident were, only that I was interested in him.

Kevin realized the danger and asked me to not pursue Tom as he was working in the same office. This made a lot of sense and I diverted my attention elsewhere. However, as time went by and Kevin became increasingly irritable even at work, Tom once came to the house while Kevin was out of town on business. You know what happened …

we had sex and it was most satisfying for me so we kept on seeing one another.

Tom fell for me and one day declared his love for me. I did not know what to do. You see, for me it was never about love. His declaration changed our relationship and I broke it off. I did not want a love affair; all I needed was relief. I loved Kevin and he was my husband and I was not going to cheat on him.

I did not see Tom again until he came to the house the morning Kevin died. Looking at him, I realized that his feelings for me had not changed, but I did not know what to do. My mind was elsewhere and I did not want to deal with him. Maybe here, with you, I will be able to clarify some issues in my mind, things that have haunted me for a long time. I am really grateful to you, Ernestine, for taking me to this magical place where I can rest from the world and make some hard decisions for my future."

Ernestine just looked at her friend and nodded gravely. "You have all the time you need and I will not intrude on your privacy, you know that, don't you?"

"I do; and I appreciate you not asking me questions. I will tell you when I am ready and have made up my mind."

The two women fell silent and watched the sun setting in the west. Ernestine turned on the little lamp on the side table and leafed through a magazine when Mary-Ann said:

"I think I will go to bed and have a good night's sleep. Talking to you has brought up some things that I want to think about. Good night, Ernestine."

"Good night, Mary-Ann."

Ernestine stayed in the living room looking out at the dark waters and the waves that kept coming and coming, never-ending. She thought about what Mary-Ann had just told her and wondered what demons her friend had to fight. She just hoped that when the time came and they had to go back that Mary-Ann will have won some of her battles.

Ernestine

Ernestine stood up and opened the door and stood on the terrace, scanning the horizon and the sky for any signs. But there were none. Slowly, she turned and closed the door behind her. Quietly, she went to her room, undressed and slid under the covers and fell into a dreamless sleep.

Chapter 15
Eric's Decision

Eric had attended Kevin's funeral but kept away from Ernestine. He could not bear to see her so close and yet unattainable for him. The morning after he had come home from Sao Paulo and found Ernestine gone, while he had taken Tuesday for a long walk, had shattered his belief in his ability to keep a relationship going.

He was furious with Ernestine for not giving him the chance to explain the situation with Tara. He was deeply disappointed in Ernestine for leaving him like that. Yet at the same time he had to admit that it was his own fault, not Ernestine's. She owed him no explanation. It was only in his mind and heart that she belonged to him. He could have followed her and explained, but his pride was badly hurt. And now, it was too late.

He was standing outside the bungalows that served as offices in the Australian outback. He had accepted the two-year assignment after Kevin's funeral and had left immediately for Sydney without leaving word with anyone. He had found a good place for Tuesday and promised to come back for her once he returned to Oregon.

He covered up the furniture, brought the food to the local shelter, and had Ernestine's things sent to her in San Diego. He had taken one last look at his cabin where he had been so happy the past few months and where he had hoped to start a new life with Ernestine. When the cab arrived, he was ready and did not look back. For him, this chapter of his life was closed.

Chapter 16
The End of a Life Chapter

Mary-Ann and Ernestine spent the days lying on the beach, driving around the island, reading and talking. One day, they watched a little crab scurrying sideways across the hot sand. Its black eyes, sticking out from the top of its head like a pin from a yellowed pin cushion. Suddenly, it stood very still observing its surroundings, and once in a while it seemed to wink at the two women. It dribbled in the sand, and with its white-gloved front pincers ate its food very daintily.

Another day they drove to the Cavernas de Camuy where they spent a few hours exploring the cool caverns formed by the river passing through it. It was a lovely drive through the lush countryside and both Ernestine and Mary-Ann had forgotten their sorrows for a few hours. They seemed almost light-hearted. They had dinner at the resort next door with its palm groves decorated with Christmas lights, curvy swimming pools with waterfalls, and food that was delicious.

The days were a string of endless hours wanting to be filled with meaning. The night before they were to leave the island, Mary-Ann confided her plans to Ernestine. She had made some hard decisions and Ernestine was astonished at her friend's courage and decisiveness.

Contrary to herself, Mary-Ann had mapped out her future life and Ernestine was sure she was going to stick to her plans. First, she was going to give leave at Scripps Hospital La Jolla, then she was going to sell her house, store her things, and go work for the Peace Corps. She told Ernestine:

"I can no longer live in San Diego where everything reminds me of Kevin and our life together. I need space and anonymity. I need to work; that will take my mind off other things."

When Ernestine asked about Tom, she replied:

"He too is a thing of the past. Seeing him brings back painful memories of Kevin and I just don't want to deal with it any longer."

"Won't you be lonely without anyone you know?"

"No, I have been often very lonely among huge crowds so it is nothing new to me. In fact, different surroundings help enormously."

She looked straight into Ernestine's eyes and said:

"The only regret I have and will always have is that I have to leave you behind. We could have been great friends until old age."

Ernestine swallowed hard and tried to stem the tears that were welling up in her eyes. She never thought that Mary-Ann would disappear from her life. She had always been such a comfort to her.

"Will you at least send an email once in a while so I know you are still among the living?" asked Ernestine sadly.

"Of course, my pet," Mary-Ann smiled. "I will even visit you when possible." With these words, she stood up, embraced Ernestine, and went to bed.

Ernestine just stood there as if nailed to the floor. Her thoughts were spinning in her head and she felt the screams of frustration at the back of her throat. Oh, how she wished Jonathan was here. But when she tried to picture his beloved face, another emerged from the depths of her mind: Eric.

In an instant she realized that her heart was trying to tell her something. Something she had desperately tried to keep away. And like the cold waves swallow a sinking ship on the vast ocean, all of her loneliness and confusion engulfed her in one upsurge of devouring yearning.

Her slim body was shaking uncontrollably and she held onto the table, knuckles white, and her breath came in little gasps. How long she had been standing there she did not know, but when the emotions finally let her go, she was drenched in sweat and as tired as if she had run for miles carrying a heavy backpack.

She looked around her with unseeing eyes and picked up the glasses, put them in the sink, and went to her bedroom. She tried to sleep but the thoughts crowded her mind, jumping relentlessly from Jonathan to Eric like children playing hop-scotch, never remaining in one place but continuously going forward toward a goal hidden behind a thick, black fog of despair. Ernestine tossed and turned until sleep finally had pity on her and she slept a dreamless sleep.

Morning came quickly and the women packed the car and drove silently back to San Juan where they caught a late flight to San Diego. As usual, the flight was uneventful and when they landed at San Diego airport, they were exhausted, physically and mentally.

To their surprise, Tom was there to take them home. He first dropped off Ernestine and then took Mary-Ann home. Ernestine felt sorry for Tom and his unrequited love for Mary-Ann and wondered if she was going to tell him tonight.

Chapter 17
Tom

When Ernestine entered her apartment she found the entryway full of boxes, and checking the label she realized that these were the things she had left at Eric's. She looked for a note but found none and was intrigued that Eric had sent her things without even getting in touch with her first. She had intended to return to Oregon after this trip and inquire about his relationship with Tara.

"Well, I shall call him in the morning and figure it out," she mumbled to herself and went to her bedroom to sleep. This time she was asleep as soon as her head touched the soft pillow.

Early next morning, she awakened and all the unanswered questions poured into her head again.

"I will call Eric first. He is up by now as Tuesday needs to go out."

She dialed his number and a recording told her that the number was disconnected. She redialed but again the recording came on. Maybe he has changed the number, so she called information but they told her that there was no telephone registered in the name of Eric Massey.

"That is strange," she thought and dialed the drugstore in town. All she could gather from the clerk was that Mr. Massey had left town, closed the house, and given the dog to a family to take care of until his return; but nobody knew where he had gone.

Then she dialed Eric's work and was told that he no longer worked for them. Ernestine was stunned. She wondered what had happened after she had left and assumed that he must have left with Tara for some unknown destination. The thought of losing him brought a sharp pain to Ernestine's heart and tears started to flow down her cheeks.

"Please, dear God, tell me that he has not vanished from my life?"

The sudden realization that she might have lost him before she even could tell him about her innermost feelings shattered her fragile hold on reality and she slumped onto the floor in a heap, crying soundlessly.

Slowly, slowly, her thoughts ambled back to the day he'd come to the hospital, the drive to his home in Oregon, the cheerful days they spent together, and the day Eric came home and presented her with puppy Tuesday. She could almost feel Tuesday's soft body against her and her wet nose on her skin.

A sharp searing pain of unimaginable loss deep inside her brought her out of her stupor. She slowly pulled herself up on a chair, shook her wild red hair, and was determined to build a new life for herself. Something her mother used to say to her came to her mind:

"I must lose myself in action, lest I wither in despair!"

She stepped out on the balcony and looked at the sky filled with ominous, dark clouds that mirrored her emotions:

"This is the second friend I am losing in as many days." Her thoughts were interrupted when suddenly, there was a loud thunderclap and the rain started. Thunder followed lightning and the sky turned a forbidding dark.

Ernestine had always been fascinated by thunderstorms and was watching the rain fall with a heavy heart. After what seemed to be an eternity, the sky started to clear and the sun peaked out among the clouds. Ernestine went inside and sat on the couch staring in front of her. She sat like this for a few moments and then decided to go for a walk along the pier.

She was just about to step out of the door when the phone rang. Instinctively, she went back and answered. It was Tom who asked to see her for lunch. Ernestine agreed and they met at a little café in the Gaslamp Quarter. Tom was already seated when she arrived and waved to her. He looked grim with disheveled hair and stubbles on his chin.

When he kissed Ernestine on the cheek she could smell stale alcohol. This was unusual, he normally was very well groomed, so Ernestine figured that Mary-Ann must have told him about her plans and that he had no place in them.

"Hi Tom," she chirped unconvincingly, "want to talk?"

"Hi Ernestine, yes I need to talk to someone who knows about Mary-Ann and me. I suppose you know that I love her and want to spend the rest of my life with her. I have never met a woman quite like her ... so independent, stubborn, intelligent and yet so sweet. You know about her plans for the future?"

Ernestine only nodded.

"Then you know that they do not include me."

Again Ernestine nodded.

"I cannot lose her, please help me find a way to persuade her to stay with me. I'd go anywhere with her, to the deepest and darkest jungle if that is what she wants, as long as she takes me along."

Raw hurt glittered in his dark eyes and tears glistened on his pale face. A soft gasp escaped her and she felt enormous pity for this tall, rawboned man sitting across from her, his hurt and longing lying naked in his eyes. Ernestine didn't know what to say so she just sat very still and waited. Eventually, Tom started to speak hesitantly.

"I have known Mary-Ann as a teenager in high school back in Indiana. She was quite brilliant even though she was Amish. Her parents weren't too keen on her attending a public high school but she was stubborn enough and prevailed. After graduation I lost sight of her for many years until I met her unexpectedly at a party at our offices. I was stunned at her cool and elegant appearance. Our eyes met and recognition seeped into her eyes. She came over and hugged me. She had also recognized me as the teenager she knew back home.

"We spent half the evening together talking about the past and where our lives had led us and how funny it was that our paths crossed again. She introduced me to her husband with whom I worked and the three of us enjoyed the rest of the evening together. Once in a while I would bump into her. She was like a magnet and I the nail that was invariably drawn to her.

"We found that we had many values in common and even liked the same movies and books. We started to go to the movies together and had dinner afterward in one of the intimate little restaurants in Hillcrest. Soon, I realized that she was more to me than just an old friend. I fantasized about her and the urge to touch her became almost unbearable.

"Yet I knew that she was fiercely loyal to her husband and would never cheat on him. Maybe that was part of the attraction. But anyhow, one day after the movie she declined dinner and told me that she had made special arrangements for us if I was willing to spend a couple of hours alone with her. You cannot imagine how I felt. She drove to a fancy place somewhere on Harbor Drive. The elevator took us up to a spacious apartment overlooking the bay."

At these words, Ernestine's heart missed a beat. She realized that Mary-Ann had taken Tom to her apartment and that Tom was unaware whose apartment it was. Tom had not noticed Ernestine's sudden change of eye color and continued with his story.

"We stood at the railing watching the stars, sipping ice cold champagne from crystal glasses, and I could not get enough of looking at her. When she wound her arms inside my jacket, her fingers' touch sent a shiver through me. I pulled her closer and she kissed me with a hunger that belied her outward calm. She gently guided me to a huge, soft bed and started undressing me."

Tom went on with his story but Ernestine's mind had begun to wander back to the time when she and Jonathan were lying in the huge, soft bed and Jonathan's hands were exploring the hollow of her back in a prelude of things to come.

She tried to remember the tingling of her skin and the passion that engulfed them, but the memory had become faint and a wave of sadness swept over her at the realization that she might lose the memory of these past emotions.

"Ernestine?"

She heard her name and slowly her mind found its way back to the present and her greenish eyes rested on that square jaw tensed visibly under her bold gaze. A look of tired sadness passed over his features and he apologized to Ernestine for talking only about himself.

All of a sudden, Ernestine felt the urge to hurt this man that had slept in her bed by telling him that it was her apartment where he had made love to Mary-Ann and that she only needed him for relief of her sexual tension, that she had never had any feelings for him, and only used him in a most base way. Surprised at her own viciousness, Ernestine smiled at Tom and encouraged him to continue with his story.

"I think you get the gory picture," he said. "I know that Mary-Ann does not love me the way she loved Kevin, but I had hoped that she would learn to like being with me, especially now that Kevin is gone."

Ernestine kept looking at him and thought about Eric and her love for him and how somehow everything in the past few weeks had gone wrong. She had thought she was the only one dealing with these emotions and now, across from her sat this man so utterly devastated by Mary-Ann's actions that she wondered whether the male species was really the strong one.

"I have no answer for you Tom," Ernestine replied, "and I wish there was something I could do. But you have known Mary-Ann much longer than I have and so you know that once she has made up her mind she will not change her plans. Maybe once she comes back from her assignment with the Peace Corps she might see things in a different light."

"It was good of you to listen to me Ernestine. And now I must bid you farewell." With these words, Tom got up and disappeared among the crowd.

Ernestine remained seated. She had an uneasy feeling about the whole conversation and tried to go over what was said once again. But it was useless. Her mind had wandered and she only remembered bits and pieces. She got up and strolled down Fifth Avenue toward the Convention Center and her apartment. She had not gone far when she heard a commotion behind her and somebody screaming:

"He is going to jump from the building!"

Instinctively, Ernestine knew that it was Tom. She raced back only to see a body falling and then hit the ground with a dull thud. The crowd fell silent and formed a circle around the dead man. Ernestine pushed her way through and knelt at Tom's side, tears flowing down her cheeks uncontrollably.

She held his still-warm hand and whispered, "Oh Tom, I am so sorry. I had no idea that you were on the verge of committing suicide."

Strong hands pulled her away and she faced a policeman that had been summoned.

"Do you know this guy?" he barked.

"It is, was, a friend of a friend of mine. His name is Tom."

"Please come to the station and give us the details," ordered the cop.

Ernestine was numb and followed the officer to the squad car.

"Any relatives we can notify?"

"Please call Mary-Ann Masters. Her husband worked with Tom and she will be of more help than I," whispered Ernestine.

At the station she gave Mary-Ann's phone number to a secretary who then made the call. Thirty minutes later, a stone-faced Mary-Ann sat silently beside Ernestine waiting to make her statement.

Two unsmiling interrogation officers questioned her endlessly about her relationship with Tom and why she did not alert anyone that he was suicidal. It helped very little that Ernestine tried to make them understand that she had only met Tom a few times during Kevin's funeral preparation.

When they finally were satisfied that she did not hide anything, they let her go; a police car took Ernestine home. She opened the door and entered her apartment. For the first time, she did not feel at home and she realized that she had to get away for a while. Too many painful memories chased one another in this place.

She sat down at her computer and booked a flight to London for the next day. Then she busied herself packing a few things into a suitcase, took a warm shower, and went to bed. She felt empty and drained and Tom's face haunted her dreams.

Chapter 18
Ernestine's Flight

On the overnight flight to London, Ernestine reviewed the events of the past few months and tried to make some sense of it all. Her thoughts went back to the day Mary-Ann and Kevin found her unconscious on the floor with a ruptured appendix.

The stay at the hospital from where Eric took her to Oregon where she spent happy weeks until the fragile relationship that was developing between her and Eric was shattered by Tara's unexpected appearance.

Ernestine looked back on that evening when Eric had come back from South America and had started to kiss her when Tara's high-pitched voice chilled him to his very soul. She could still feel the cold tension hanging like an ice curtain in the air and realized that she had fled from the house like a coward.

There was something important that Eric wanted to tell her. She instinctively knew that he had come to a decision involving the both of them and that she was not ready to deal with it. She knew that she had feelings for that tender teddy bear of a man with his big dark brooding eyes shining with an intense light that evening.

But to her it felt like cheating on Jonathan. Yet Jonathan would have wanted her to be happy and content again and who better than Eric, his longtime trusted friend? But she had run away from the situation instead of dealing with it and now she felt a vast emptiness in the pit of her stomach. It is one thing to lose someone due to circumstances beyond one's control, but it is quite another to run away from one's innermost feelings.

Ernestine tried to sleep but as so often happened, sleep eluded her and images were crowding her mind. She saw herself playing with Robin in the little creek behind her grandmother's house. Then she was at the reception at the Hotel Intercontinental in Chicago where she met Jonathan.

A smile softened her tired face when her thoughts brought back memories of Jonathan's courtship, their evenings together on his balcony, the first time he made love to her, and the honeymoon on the Big Island of Hawaii.

When dark images wanted to intrude, Ernestine forced herself to stay awake and started to read a novel she had picked up at the airport. It was one of those easy-to-read paperbacks that is perfect for an airplane ride. Nothing to think about and it does not matter whether one misses a few pages.

However, after a few chapters, Ernestine felt her eyes closing and the images started to flood her mind again. She remembered the day Swissair 111 crashed off the coast of Halifax and the death of her parents, the police officers that came to the house to tell her about Jonathan's accident, and Kevin's death.

When the voice over the loudspeaker asked the passengers to go back to their seats and fasten their seatbelts due to some anticipated turbulences, the images faded and Ernestine opened her eyes. The meal service was about to start and she was glad about it. The older lady sitting in the seat beside her turned toward her and said:

"At least the food is decent. Will you join me with a glass of wine?"

"Gladly," replied Ernestine.

"You must have had some beautiful dream at first but then something happened and tears were rolling down your cheeks. Are you quite all right?"

"Yes I am. I just had some rough times behind me and I hope the future is going to be brighter."

The old lady studied Ernestine's face and remarked:

"You are a beautiful woman and a gentle one too. Life has ups and downs and sometimes it not only puts stones in our way but whole high mountains. I should know. I have been there. Like my mother used to say … *Life happens when you have made other plans.*"

"How true this is," whispered Ernestine. "I have learned that lesson very painfully and now I try to avoid making plans. They usually get changed by circumstances anyway."

"Want to talk over dinner?" offered the lady.

And Ernestine began to tell her story. She did not leave anything out, nor did she embellish anything. She felt very comfortable talking to this woman with gray hair and she forgot that they were actually forty thousand feet in the air hurtling across the wide expanse of the United States and the Atlantic.

While talking, Ernestine felt a weight lifting from her shoulders and she saw her future in a brighter light. Ernestine had not realized that the dinner service had been over for several hours. Only when they were asked what they wanted for breakfast did she realize that she must have talked for hours.

"Oh, I must have bored you with my talking for this long," she apologetically said to the woman.

"Not at all. You have lived through quite a lot in a very short time and you will see that you will tackle life differently from now on ... with more respect and gratitude."

Breakfast arrived and both women silently ate their croissant and drank their tea. The announcement over the intercom told them that they were anticipating to land at Heathrow in about forty-five minutes.

Ernestine looked out the window at the English countryside she had so loved as a child. It was a rare sunny fall day and she could see the proper little row houses flanking the paved street. With little movement, the plane landed and taxied to the gate. Ernestine helped the lady get her bag down from the overhead bin and walked with her over the gangway. There, the lady gave her a hug and said:

"Now, little sparrow, smile and life will smile back at you."

Ernestine stood perfectly still and watched her walk away. Her words still in her ears: "My little sparrow." How long has it been since she had heard these words? It seemed to her forever, and yet it was just over a year ago since Jonathan had whispered them into her ear.

Somebody bumped into her with a suitcase and that jolted Ernestine out of her stupor. She started walking toward immigration and then picked up her luggage. She took a cab to her hotel right in the center of London. As a child, she had stayed with her parents at the Mayfair Hotel and had decided to stay there for a few days until she had sorted out what she wanted to do and where to go.

The cab stopped at the front entrance and a handsome bell boy helped her with the luggage and accompanied her to her room on the third floor. Ernestine handed him a bunch of dollars, took a shower, slipped between the cool satin sheets, and was asleep before she had time to unpack.

Next morning, Ernestine awoke refreshed and hungry. She showered, put on her jeans and favorite little sandals, an embroidered white t-shirt and her dark gray cardigan and went down to the lobby. It was as impressive as ever.

Ernestine walked out to the street and found a little sandwich shop in one of the side streets. She ordered an egg sandwich and a cup of hot black tea with a bit of milk. While munching on her sandwich, she was trying to figure out what she wanted to do. Now that she was in England, her life in San Diego seemed very far away indeed and she had a feeling of freedom that she had not experienced in a long, long time.

When she stepped out of the café, she spotted a drug store across the street and decided to buy a map of England.

"Maybe I'll rent a car and drive to the Lake District, or maybe to the Salisbury Plain, or maybe I should go up to Scotland," she mused. "The solitude of the Highlands might just be what I need right now to sort out my life."

She wandered along the broad streets toward Piccadilly Circus and enjoyed the feel of this vibrant city. She peeked into the big windows of the department stores on Oxford Street but did not enter the stores. She felt light and almost happy and did not want to lose this elusive feeling by being pushed around in the crowded stores.

She walked and walked until she came to Hyde Park. Only then did she realize that she must have walked for hours. She stopped at a little tea place and had a scone and black tea with milk. Memories of visits to London with her parents and grandparents flooded her mind and she leaned back on her chair and stared at the brightly-painted ceiling.

It was a very curious ceiling with greenish tiles at an angle and dark wood beams across the whole length of the room. Pretty, shiny chandeliers hung from the beams and gave the establishment a somewhat sophisticated look, had it not been for the blue plastic chairs and tables. Ernestine imagined that at one time the high society of London may have frequented this place.

Her musings were rudely interrupted when the waitress at the next table dropped a tray with dirty dishes. Ernestine got up, paid and left half her scone uneaten on the plate. When she stepped into the busy street, rain had started to fall and a sea of black umbrellas was bobbing up and down along the busy road.

Ernestine hired a cab and after a good while the driver dropped her off at the Mayfair Hotel. She went to her room and watched some television while sipping a glass of wine. Later, too tired to dress up and go out, she ordered some soup, a crab-stuffed chicken breast, and a mixed salad from room service. When the food was brought she sat down and hungrily ate the delicious meal.

Some sitcom was playing on the TV set and Ernestine watched without really seeing anything or hearing what the characters were saying. Her thoughts had traveled back in time to when she was staying with her grandparents in Chester.

She remembered the day she met Robin while trying to catch a butterfly. Her mind rested on Robin and she was wondering what he was doing at this precise moment. She had not heard from him since the day he had shown up at her door and Jonathan told her afterward that Robin was in love with her. She had not quite believed it then. The thought of Jonathan brought tears to her eyes.

"Why, why my love, did you have to go? Leave me alone in this world that is cold and unfriendly without you?"

A loud noise intruded on her and pulled her out of the somber thoughts, transporting her back to the present. It was her phone that was ringing insistently, but before she could answer, the caller had hung up. Tired, Ernestine got ready for bed hoping for a good night's sleep.

The next morning, golden sunshine flooded her room and made the dust particles sparkle like gold flakes in a bottle of water. She jumped out of bed, into the shower and decided to visit some of London's sights.

She walked along Albemarle Street, when she spotted the small gallery John Marin of London. She entered and was amazed at the variety of artists exhibited. There were the well-known ones like Miró and Kadinsky, but also artists unknown to her whose paintings she really liked. She was studying the picture hanging in front of her when a deep voice called her:

"You look pretty interested in this painting by John Constable, but I would appreciate it if you could call your boss and tell him that Lord Fairfax is here to see him."

Ernestine turned around and her eyes met the ice blue eyes of Lord Fairfax. He was of medium height, with a shock of white hair perfectly coiffed framing his suntanned face. Something in his demeanor made Ernestine uneasy and she quickly looked around, spotted a door with "Private" written on it and headed toward it at a fast pace. Once inside, she took a deep breath and stepped into the dim sunlight, shining through a grimy window.

"Who the heck are you?" barked a voice from some dark corner. "Are you illiterate? There is a big sign reading *Private* on the door you just came through and you may just go out that way again."

"Lord Fairfax is in the gallery and wants to see you," Ernestine replied quietly.

"Are you his new secretary or what?"

"No, he mistook me as your assistant and I saw no harm in playing that role for a few minutes. Now, had I known that you are such a grouch I may have told him that you were unavailable for any Lords or Ladies for that matter."

With these words, Ernestine turned around and made for the door. But before she could reach it, a hand pulled on her arm and a much gentler voice said:

"Forgive me. My behavior toward you was inexcusable; but if you give me a chance I will explain to you after I have attended to Lord Fairfax. Have a seat, I shan't be too long."

With these words, the unknown man went through the door, leaving Ernestine behind. She had no intention of waiting for this rude person and opened the door just enough to overhear the two men whispering something about Constable's paintings. She could not make out enough to understand what was going on and decided on the spur of the moment to wait and see how this all would develop.

After not more than twenty minutes, the sourly man came back with a big smile on his face.

"You did it, you, you person you. What is your name anyway?"

"Ernestine."

"Good solid name. I like it. Lord Fairfax was very impressed with your obedience and promised to sell me one or two of John Constable's lost paintings. Please sit down and we shall have some tea and we shall talk."

He rang for tea and like magic, two white porcelain cups and saucers arrived on a beautifully-painted tray together with a steaming hot pot of tea and sweet-smelling scones. Ernestine realized that she was actually hungry and was happy to listen to the little man tell his story while she nibbled on her scones and sipped the hot, flavorful tea.

His name was Mr. Fisher, Abraham Fisher. He had inherited the gallery from his father who had passed away some years ago. Mr. Fisher had tried to make something of the gallery but had been unsuccessful until the day Lord Fairfax came to his place of business.

Lord Fairfax had been looking all over London for a John Constable painting that had belonged to his family and had been pawned by one of his cousins some years ago. The cousin had passed away and no pawn shop had any records of this painting. It was the forerunner to "Brighton Beach."

On this particular autumn afternoon, Lord Fairfax spotted the little gallery tucked away on Albemarle Street and on impulse entered the establishment. He was overwhelmed when the first thing he saw was the long-lost Constable painting. He bought it on the spot for a very handsome sum of money and had become a loyal customer ever since.

"You know, he has been asking me to hire an assistant but I have refused. There is not enough to do for two people here, but since he thinks that I have finally given in to his request and hired an assistant, I wonder if you would take the position?"

Ernestine was taken aback, but after a few moments said:

"I think I would like that, Mr. Fisher. I shall come back tomorrow afternoon as your assistant."

With these words, Ernestine bid Mr. Fisher good-bye and left the gallery.

She strolled along the cobblestoned streets to Regent Street, deep in thought. I have nothing more important to do. I might as well become Mr. Fisher's gallery assistant. She smiled and mused at how fate has thrown her a lifeline when she most needed it.

In her head she made plans of how she was going to be a working woman. Before she realized it, she was at the door of her hotel and quickly went to her room. She opened her laptop and started a search for an apartment close to the gallery. It would be more convenient to live in her own place rather than a hotel.

She spent a couple of hours trying to find something and finally gave up. I need a realtor who can help me with this. She then ordered some dinner, stuffed salmon with baby spinach, and ate in her room. Before she fell asleep she realized that she did not even know when she was supposed to be at the gallery. She set her little red alarm clock at 8 o'clock and figured that she would be at her new work place by opening time.

Chapter 19
Eventful London

Mr. Fisher's gallery turned out to be a treasure trove. Ernestine found painting after painting in storage boxes and began to unpack them. Most were already framed with gilded frames and small white tags declaring their provenance. There were old masters and contemporary artists, huge paintings for big empty walls and miniature ones for intimate bathrooms.

She started to sort them by size and age, and after a few weeks the gallery looked quite impressive. Mr. Fisher was pleased to have found an assistant with so much zeal and was content to let her rearrange the gallery.

Ernestine had finally hired a real estate agent and spent most weekends looking at flats. Eventually, she found a small, one-bedroom flat on Maddox Street in a beautifully-restored old building with wrought iron fencing. The flat boasted high ceilings, narrow floor-to-ceiling windows and wooden floors.

Ernestine liked the open white kitchen with black granite countertops, the bedroom with built-in closets, and the modern bathroom with its glass sink. The furniture was contemporary, off-white and looked new.

She immediately signed the contract for six months and was handed the key. She went back to her hotel, collected her few belongings and checked out. The clerk smiled sadly at her and wished her a pleasant day.

Arriving at her new place, Ernestine looked around and made a list of things she would need immediately, such as linens, dishes, pots and pans and some groceries. She found a Tesco nearby and bought some milk, butter, tea, and some ginger snaps.

She hailed a cab and asked the driver to get her to a Selfridges' department store. There, she purchased a set of pale teal sheets and some kitchen towels with sunflowers on it. Another cab brought her back to her new flat. She carried the bags upstairs, opened the windows, and let the cool air come in while she made the bed and arranged her groceries in the refrigerator.

She had a glass of milk with some ginger snaps for dinner and went to bed early. When she awoke next morning, the sunshine was streaming into her bedroom and she felt happy for the first time in a very long time.

The next few weeks passed quickly and Ernestine decorated the flat with colorful paintings she had found at the Portobello Road market, red and black earthen pottery that she saw in a store window on a narrow side street, and fresh flowers. She liked her place and it began to feel like home to her.

One afternoon after she had locked the gallery, she decided to have a drink at the Coach and Horses Pub. It was a beautiful Tudor-style building. Its dark wood beams gleamed in the sun and the whitewashed walls were spotless. Baskets with vibrant flowers hung from the windowsills and muted conversations drifted through the open windows to the street.

Ernestine pushed the heavy wooden door and entered. Inside, she had to wait for her eyes to adjust to the diffused light before she could look around and find a seat. Her eyes swept the room and stopped at a table with a handsome, dark-haired man who stared at her. She was about to turn away when the stranger softly called, "Ernestine?"

She spun around and looked more closely at the man and then a big smile illuminated her face:

"Robin!" she exclaimed, and ran to his table. "What a coincidence to find you here! Are you on vacation? Or on a business trip? Oh please, talk to me."

Robin smiled, invited her to sit, took her hand, and kissed it lightly.

"Lovely to meet you here; what an utter surprise. You are the last person I expected to find here. Life is really very quirky, isn't it?"

"Yes, it is," replied Ernestine, happy to see her old childhood friend again. "But tell me, what brings you to London? I seem to remember that you would avoid the city at all costs, no?"

"Yes, I try hard not to be forced to come here, but this is something that could not be avoided." A deep crease inserted itself between his lovely gray eyes and gave his face a spoiled look. "To make a very long and hurtful story very short, I am here to meet my father for the first time."

Ernestine gasped. "You mean to say that your father is not your father? I mean, there is someone else? Tell me please, but only if you want to," she added, seeing his frown deepening.

"There is not much to tell, but I shall try. Some time ago I received a letter from a prestigious solicitor's firm asking me politely to come to London at my earliest convenience to discuss a rather delicate matter. You can imagine that I was intrigued by this letter and telephoned the solicitor. He would not give me any answers and only reiterated his request for me to come to his London office at my convenience.

"We set an appointment three weeks from that day and I travelled to London. At the solicitor's, I was asked to identify myself and tell them about my childhood … who my parents were, where I spent the summers, the schools I had attended, and what I was doing now. The solicitor listened to all my talk and at the end took a file from his desk, opened it, looked at me with his bespectacled eyes and said, 'Mr. Whittaker was not your biological father. However, Mrs. Whittaker is your mother. She had a boy out of wedlock and the marriage to Mr. Whittaker was arranged to avoid a scandal.'

"You cannot imagine what I felt when this aloof solicitor told me this to my face. I jumped out of my seat and would have hit him had I not stumbled and fallen to my knees. I was so humiliated, and stormed out of his office into the London traffic.

"After having marched around for a good half hour, I returned to his office where I found him still seated looking at the file. Without hesitation, he continued and told me that I was to meet my father today, here. He also told me the circumstances of my adoption and my father's name.

"At first, I did not want anything to do with this man who not only had abandoned me but also my mother. But the solicitor was very persuasive and at the end I agreed to meet this man. All I really know is that he is a Lord, owns a country manor somewhere, and loves to visit a gallery at Albemarle Street."

Ernestine looked away and thoughts raced through her mind ... Lord Fairfax Robin's father? She realized she had to leave before Lord Fairfax came and recognized her. She did not wish to be drawn into this very private matter between these two men.

She looked at her watch and said, "Robin, I completely forgot my appointment. I have to leave but please can we meet later on or tomorrow? Here is my phone number, you can call me anytime."

She kissed him lightly on the cheek, turned, and left the pub without giving Robin a chance to say something.

She walked to her flat, let herself in, got a cold Diet Coke from the fridge, and sat down on the soft couch with the many-colored pillows. She closed her eyes and tried to force Mr. and Mrs. Whittaker's faces into her consciousness. She somewhat succeeded and she tried to find some traits Robin had inherited from his mother. However, she was unsuccessful. Too much time had passed since she last saw them one summer many, many years ago, before they had moved away.

Ernestine reviewed in her mind days that were somehow special and had stayed with her since her childhood. Her reverie was interrupted by the shrill sound of the telephone. She answered the call and it was Robin.

"Hey you, running out on me like this at a time when I could really have used a friend," he complained. "Will you have dinner with me tonight? I'll pick you up in about an hour, provided you give me your address."

Ernestine gave him the address and hung up. She went to her closet and carefully chose an outfit … black slacks, a sea blue light sweater, and her Italian sandals. She put a necklace with small black pearls around her neck and stared at herself in the mirror.

She had not worn the pearls since Jonathan had died. They had been a gift from him when he came back from a trip to Tahiti. Tears welled in her eyes and threatened to smear her make-up. The joy of having dinner with her old friend went out of her and if she had known how to reach him she would have cancelled and instead crawled into bed to cry.

At that moment, the doorbell rang and Ernestine had no more time to take off her pearls or to wallow in self-pity. She opened the door and there was Robin, tall and handsome as ever. Age had been especially kind to him and he looked better than she could remember. His face creased with some wrinkles that gave it character and his gray eyes shone like dark puddles in the sunlight.

"Hi again," he said while he pulled her into his arms. "Thanks for accepting dinner with me. It has been far too long and we have loads to talk about. Anything particular you feel like eating tonight?"

Ernestine shook her head and Robin took her arm and guided her to the elevator.

"Let's go to Patterson's on Mill Street. I am sure you will find something you like."

They quickly walked down Maddox Street and entered Patterson's restaurant. They were seated by a large window overlooking the square. A waiter dressed in black and white brought them the menu and said, "I will be back in a few minutes to take your order."

Both Ernestine and Robin looked at the menu and made mental notes. When the waiter came back they were ready to order. Ernestine ordered a roasted lobster salad for starters, filet of Scottish beef with shallot comfit, spinach, chips and wine jus for the entrée. Robin ordered warm beef Carpaccio in mushroom tea for starters and sea bass with black squid rice, calamari, whitebait and pesto.

While waiting for the food to arrive, they talked about long-forgotten times when their worlds were still small and their hearts innocent without having known any pain.

The food arrived and it was as delicious as it sounded. Ernestine enjoyed herself thoroughly. Robin was an exceptional companion and the time just flew by. After paying the bill, they were both reluctant to end the evening and Ernestine hesitated to invite Robin back to her place.

But then she looked at him sidewise and saw the honesty in his face, his eyes looking at her the same way they used to look so many summers ago when he told her that catching butterflies was cruel.

Ernestine chuckled and Robin turned his head to fully look at her. Ernestine said, "Let's go for a cup of tea at my place. I probably have some forgotten cookies in a cupboard that are waiting to be devoured."

"Sounds like a good idea. Let's go."

He took her arm and they strolled back along Maddox to her apartment where Ernestine made tea but did not find the cookies. Sitting in comfortable chairs facing the big window, they remembered their childhood and the long-gone summers they spent together as children. Ernestine briefly told him about Jonathan's accident, the time she spent with Mary-Ann, the death of Kevin and then Tom, and how this had wrecked her friendship with Mary-Ann. Robin told her about his travel and work, some girlfriends, and the encounter with Lord Fairfax.

"I bet you would like to hear about my encounter with my *father*," teased Robin.

"Only if you want to talk about it," replied Ernestine.

"Well, let me see. You had just left, when this older man with white hair came over to my table and introduced himself as Lord Fairfax. He sat down, ordered a cup of tea and started to talk about how he had met my mother.

"His family owned an estate close to Chester and my mother was one of the scullery maids. She was very pretty with her long black hair, huge sad gray eyes, and a pouting rose button for a mouth. Lord Fairfax, well he was not a lord then, fell in love with her lovely little face and my mother was too young and inexperienced to resist very long.

"One summer evening, they were walking along the river Dee that was once an important seaway and the foundation for Chester's fortune, when Lord Fairfax proposed to my mother. She accepted and they proceeded back to the house and told his parents about this glorious event.

"They did not at all anticipate the furor, anger and disappointment of his parents. My mother was ordered to immediately leave her employment and never come back, and Lord Fairfax was sent abroad the next day. They had no way of communicating with one another and lost contact for many years.

"In the meantime, as you can imagine, my mother found out that she was pregnant with me. She found a nice couple that needed a live-in companion and when I was born, they became my grandparents. My mother never told me who my father was, only that he had no interest in her and did not know of my existence. This has never bothered me as my mother loved me more than I can tell you.

"Anyhow, when the old Lord Fairfax died, my father became Lord and moved back to his estate. He had made a fortune in Australia, was married to an Australian woman, and when she passed away around the same time as his father, he decided to return to England. He hired a detective to find my mother but to his surprise, he found a son."

During his speech, Robin had clenched and unclenched his hands to disguise the emotions that swept through him. Ernestine sat there looking at him and waiting for him to break the silence. She could see that his thoughts had taken him far away from here, back to his childhood, trying to find an indication that this Lord was really his father.

"I am not very good company tonight, Ernestine, and if you don't mind I will go and hopefully we can repeat dinner some other evening when I have less on my mind."

"You have my phone number. Call me anytime," replied Ernestine quietly.

Robin got up, collected his belongings, kissed her absentmindedly on her cheek, and left. Ernestine watched him leave the building and cross the empty street. She slowly turned around and sat down in her favorite chair and let her thoughts race toward the past. She did not know how long she had been sitting like that when suddenly her phone rang pulling her out of her thoughts. For a split second she hoped it would be Robin, but it was a wrong number.

"Well," she said to herself, "I might as well go to bed now that I am awake." She slipped between the sheets and fell into a restless sleep.

Chapter 20
A Drive in the Countryside

Next morning, when Ernestine left her building there was a slight chill in the air. She pulled her pastel cardigan closer around her and accelerated her steps. Winter is approaching rapidly, she thought, and was looking forward to visiting the colorful woods outside London.

Arriving at the gallery, she was surprised to see Robin there.

"Hi Robin, are you waiting for me?"

"Actually, Lord Fairfax, ehm, my father, is inside and I am waiting for him to finish his business and then drive to his estate in the West Midlands."

"Lucky you, to escape to the countryside, while I am slaving away here. But anyway, I better go inside before your father comes out and sees us chatting like old friends." Ernestine smiled. She turned and opened the door when Robin called to her:

"Why don't you come with us to the countryside? I am sure Mr. Fisher would not dare object you going away for a few days with Lord Fairfax, and I could certainly use your company."

"What about your father, Robin?" Ernestine asked. "Might he not perceive me as an intruder when you and he are going to his estate for the first time together? I do not wish to be in the way."

"Silly girl," Robin said and drew her closer, "*I* am sure he will not mind taking his favorite gallery assistant with him on this trip."

Before Ernestine could answer, the door opened and Lord Fairfax stood there, imposing in his dark gray tailored suit and his white hair. He took one look at Robin and Ernestine and a big smile traveled all over his face.

"Well, well, you do not waste any time Robin, to meet exquisite women."

"May I present Ernestine Leclerc; she is a childhood friend of mine. We met again a few days ago quite by chance."

"I have met Ernestine. She is a treasure and has transformed this gallery into a gem." Turning to Ernestine, he said, "You being a friend of Robin's, why don't you join us on our trip to the West Midlands? I am sure Robin would be delighted to have you join us."

"That is just fine with me," peeped Mr. Fisher from the open door. "I will close the gallery until you are back." With these words he disappeared into the foyer and closed the door.

Ernestine looked from Robin to Lord Fairfax and smiled. "Well, I guess I am outnumbered here and I better pack some things and join you in about one hour."

"We'll pick you up at the apartment," Robin answered, and his dark gray eyes sparkled with pleasure.

Ernestine quickly walked back to her place, took some clothes out of the closet and put them on the bed, when suddenly she realized that she had not a clue what she was supposed to be wearing. She had never been invited to a Lord's estate before and was very unfamiliar with the expected etiquette.

Finally, she decided on some dark slacks that could be worn with high-heeled shoes or walking shoes, a few blouses in different colors, light sweaters and her new, beige parka. She was ready by the time Robin rang the doorbell.

After her luggage was stored in the trunk, the chauffeur opened the door of the dark brown Bentley and she found herself sitting beside Lord Fairfax. Robin was facing her. Slowly, the car moved into traffic and merged onto the motorway. The ride was smooth and the three passengers talked about this and that.

The six-hour drive ended when they arrived at the Fairfax estate. Ernestine was greeted by a beautifully-restored country house. The main entrance was framed by two-story bay windows with three plate-glass sashes. The gleaming tile roof reflected the last sunrays of the day; and the trees were in full fall color.

Lord Fairfax bid them to enter and their luggage was taken upstairs to their rooms. Ernestine found herself in a beautifully-appointed bedroom suite, complete with a fireplace, sitting area, bedroom and full bathroom. The colors were kept in crèmes and pastel greens. The floor-to-ceiling windows were covered with cream-colored sheers and drapes of a velvety fairy green.

The carpet was a plush soft forest green, reminding Ernestine of the Chester forest in spring when the world was slowly awakening to the warm spring sun. The two deep chairs were covered with a crème and green-striped damask with matching pillows. The bedspread was a creamy silk, and Ernestine was looking forward to slipping between the sheets and having a good night's sleep.

Presently, there was a knock on her door and she heard Robin's voice:

"Ernestine, come let's go and explore the surroundings before the sun sets completely. I was told that the view from the little hill is quite spectacular."

Ernestine opened the door and went with Robin to climb the hill. Once on top, the view took their breath away. As far as one could see there were the famed rolling hills of England and the Welsh mountains to the west. The setting sun painted long shadows on the gentle slopes and everything was bathed in an autumn glow where the white clouds in the sky looked somewhat out of place.

Both Ernestine and Robin were taken aback by this view and silently they looked around, each absorbed in their own thoughts. Suddenly, the silence was broken by

Lord Fairfax's voice saying, "It is quite stunning this view isn't it?"

"It is absolutely gorgeous," replied Ernestine, "so peaceful, and the smell of heather is quite lovely. Now I understand why people fall in love with the English countryside."

Lord Fairfax nodded and took her arm leading her down the hill. Robin followed a few steps behind watching his father and Ernestine walking toward the house.

Dinner was ready to be served in the dining room, a high-ceilinged pleasant room with a long wooden table at its center, exquisite mahogany sideboards along the walls laden with plates, covered platters and crystal glasses. Ernestine liked what she saw and at the request of the Lord sat down on the appointed chair that was covered in red and teal-striped brocade. A servant brought her a hot wet towel to clean her hands.

Lord Fairfax spotted her puzzled look at this and before she could ask answered:

"I like the custom in airplanes where a towel is brought before each meal."

Ernestine nodded in agreement and another servant put a plate of steaming soup on her charger plate. The steam swirled up and it smelled delicious. The soup was followed by a plate of roasted beef, herbed potatoes and different vegetables. They ate in silence; and when the last silver knife and fork was put down, Lord Fairfax invited them to the library for tea.

Ernestine had never seen such a library. Dark bookshelves lined the walls from floor to ceiling, interrupted only by huge windows. The books were nicely aligned and there were books that looked very old with dark brown leather jackets and others wore the bright colors of today's book jackets. Ernestine slowly walked along the walls gazing at this treasure trove of collected knowledge.

"How Jonathan would have loved to spend time here, browsing and reading selected pages," she thought. Her sparkling green eyes lost her sparkle as she remembered him and realized that he would always be a part of her, yet never talk to her again; no more awakening in his arms after a night of lovemaking; no more discussions about the genius of humankind or the lack thereof; no more laughter together at some private joke.

"Are you alright?' said a voice close to her.

She turned and looked into the gray serious eyes of Robin.

"Yes, I am fine," she lied and continued her walk along the bookcases. She wiped her eyes and forced herself to come back to the present and to leave the thoughts of Jonathan for a lonely night.

"Tea is served," announced the butler and they sat down in the comfortable reading chairs set around a low coffee table decorated with a multitude of lit candles in all shapes and forms. They gave off a pleasant smell of apples and woods and their diffused light turned the library into a theater of shadows.

The butler lit the fire in the huge fireplace in the corner and the shadows started their dance on the walls. Fascinated, Ernestine watched their endless moves and her eyes slowly started to close. A dream formed but the voice of Lord Fairfax called her back to the library.

"It has been a long day for all of us and I think that Ernestine is ready to call it quits."

Ernestine agreed, got up, bid good night to both men, and went to her room. Once between the sheets, it took only a few minutes for her to fall asleep.

Chapter 21
A Morning Ride

The next morning saw a golden dawn spread over the land. Ernestine stretched herself like a kitten and slowly crept out of the huge bed. She padded to the window and opened the heavy curtain. "This is magnificent," she thought, and for a moment seemed to feel Jonathan's touch on her cheek, but it was only a warm sunray.

"I wish you were here, my beloved, to delight in this with me." Ernestine stared with unseeing eyes at the world outside her window while tears slowly trickled down her warm cheeks. A knock at her door pulled her out of her daze and transported her back to the manor house.

Robin's voice was calling for her, letting her know that breakfast was going to be served within the hour. Quickly, Ernestine took a shower, donned black slacks and her pale green silk blouse, applied light make-up and was ready in half an hour.

She descended the wide staircase and followed the muffled voices to a pleasant room where breakfast was served. Lord Fairfax and Robin were seated at a large round table with a view of the gardens. Steaming cups of very black tea were served and Ernestine savored the lavish English breakfast.

There were eggs any style, freshly-baked breads, muffins and rolls, homemade jams, jellies, and marmalade, creamy butter churned at the estate, and hash browns with tiny bits of crispy bacon.

Presently, Lord Fairfax was saying. "I would like to show you the estate this morning and then you two can roam around in the afternoon while I have to attend a meeting in the village."

Both Ernestine and Robin agreed; and after they had finished with their breakfast, they joined Lord Fairfax in the courtyard. Three excellent horses were brought to them, already saddled and ready to mount. Lord Fairfax saw the puzzled look on Robin's and Ernestine's faces and laughingly asked, "You do ride, don't you?"

"Well," answered Robin, "I used to ride when I was a boy, but it has been many years since I last rode a horse."

"And you, Ernestine?"

"I used to ride with my husband along the beaches in Rosarito when he was still with me," Ernestine replied quietly.

"Her husband passed away a couple of years ago," Robin said. "… a car accident."

"I see," said Lord Fairfax; and turning to Ernestine took her hand and said, "I am sorry for your loss, my dear. Anything Robin and I can do, we will."

With these words he mounted his horse and trotted out of the courtyard.

"Are you up to a little ride, Ernestine?" asked Robin.

"Yes," and she mounted the white horse ready for her. Robin followed suit and the three of them left the house and rode at a fair pace toward a little forest not too far away.

"We shall ride along the perimeter of the estate so you get an idea of the size of the estate," explained Lord Fairfax.

They rode in silence for some time, each one of them occupied with their own thoughts. It was one of those rare fall mornings when the sun makes the air shimmer and the morning dew can still be seen on the green grass and colored leaves. The horses' breaths looked like dancing spirits, and Ernestine felt at peace in this magical place.

They climbed a short hill where some men were fixing a broken wooden fence and stopped at a little stone outcropping. There they dismounted and Lord Fairfax showed them the estate. Across from where they stood they could see the country house with its many smoking chimneys. To the left were large meadows framed by forests, and to the right one could just spot a silver ribbon, the river Arrow.

Using his outstretched arm sweeping over the countryside, Lord Fairfax said, "Once all this land belonged to our ancestors. It got sold bit by bit until my grandfather kept it the way it is still today. You can see the different fences and forests along the borders. It is still one of the larger holdings in the area, but obviously it has lost a lot from its glory days."

Robin and Ernestine followed his gaze and were amazed at the beauty of the place.

"Why do you ever come to London?" asked Ernestine, "I think I would just stay here and take pleasure in these peaceful and magnificent surroundings."

"Business takes me more often to London than I care for," replied the Lord, then turned around and mounted his dark stallion.

Robin and Ernestine followed suit and silently they kept riding through the morning mist. When they arrived back at the manor, stable boys took care of the reigns and led the horses away to be fed and watered.

"I have to attend to some matters," Lord Fairfax said, "so you two are free to do whatever you feel like. You can go to town or explore the manor. There are many rooms that are hardly used and you might want to choose some for you when you are staying here. Anything you wish can be brought here from somewhere." With these words, the lord disappeared behind a big gilded oak door.

"Want to go to the village, look at rooms, explore the grounds, or read by the fireplace?" Robin asked.

"I think I'll read for a while. I need to digest all these beautiful views, and the ride also tired me. I am not used to horseback riding."

"Alright, I'll see you in a couple of hours for lunch."

Ernestine mounted the stairs to her beautiful room and looked around in amazement. The previous night upon her arrival she had not really looked about the room, and this morning she was busy getting dressed to avoid being late for breakfast.

It was a bright and airy room with tall windows overlooking the meadows and forests. Soft cream-colored sheers were blowing in the breeze and the heavy velvet curtains stood like soldiers at attention on either side of the windows. The wallpaper, in beige and gold tones, complemented the particular creamy hue of the silk bedspread.

The dark hardwood floors were waxed to a shine and a thick forest-green woolen carpet covered some of it. The nightstands, dresser and writing table were a rich mahogany. The writing table faced the window, where the natural light gave it an inviting atmosphere and tempted one to write letters.

Two deep comfortable grandfather chairs were perfectly arranged by the old brick fireplace. A fire had been lit and the warmth emanating from it felt good on Ernestine's cold cheeks. She looked around and saw quite a collection of small paintings by renowned English painters and one big one over the bed by John Constable. Ernestine thought it was the "Evening Landscape of East Bergholt."

"I have to ask Lord Fairfax about this one," she thought, walking toward the window. The whitish sun stood high in the sky and the early morning clouds had fled before its rays. The landscape looked clean, in order, and at peace. She closed the window, grabbed a book that had been left on the window sill, sat down in one of the soft chairs and started to read. It was not long before her eyes closed and dreams invaded her slumber.

A hard knock at the door woke her up and it took her a moment to realize where she was when she heard Robin's voice:

"Suri, come let's have some lunch and then go to the village for a stroll around the commons. It is such a lovely afternoon."

"Coming, just give me a moment," replied Ernestine and opened the door for her friend. She was taken aback by his looks. His gray eyes were sparkling like a lake in the moonlight and a boyish smile played around his full lips. He was dressed in tight-fitting blue jeans, white shirt and black blazer.

"You want to break all the girls' hearts in the village, looking like this?" Ernestine asked with a mischievous smile.

"Nope, I only want yours," Robin replied, looking all of a sudden very serious.

Ernestine turned and looked at him and saw the change in him immediately. "I have to be careful; he is very attractive and a Lord's son," but she did not say anything. Instead, she grabbed the little beige cardigan that was draped over the back of the sofa and followed Robin downstairs.

Lunch was served on the terrace and both Robin and Ernestine realized that they were hungry. The morning ride had taken its toll. After the delicious lunch, they asked the driver to drop them off at the village commons and wait for them.

They shopped in the little boutiques and curio stores that lined the commons. Ernestine found a small greenish perfume bottle like the one her grandmother used to have and Robin bought it for her.

"A little gift, so you will think of me," he said, "whenever you see it."

Ernestine thanked him and was wondering what this was all about. She did not want to speculate and knew that she would never be ready for Robin.

When dark clouds swept in from the west, they decided to go back. They had hardly gotten into the

Bentley, when the rain started to fall. First, in big, slow drops, and then harder and harder. Thunderclaps could be heard in the distance and the sky was lit with lightning. They made it safely back to the manor where they would meet Lord Fairfax for dinner.

At the table, Lord Fairfax inquired about their day and they had a lively conversation about this and that. It was decided that all would drive back the next day as Lord Fairfax had to be in the city unexpectedly. Ernestine was glad to return and put some distance between herself and Robin.

Early the next morning, they left for London. The drive was uneventful and Ernestine was dropped off at her flat. She climbed the stairs to her apartment and went straight to bed even though it was only late afternoon. Sleep eluded her for a couple of hours but then she fell into a dreamless sleep.

Chapter 22
Mr. Fisher's Legacy

Ernestine went to work listlessly. The sky hung deep and ominous black clouds slowly glided above. Ernestine pulled her stylish raincoat closer trying to keep the dampness out. Luckily she arrived at the gallery before the sky opened to a torrential rain that belted the city's sidewalks and anyone still out in the open.

Mr. Fisher was busy in his storeroom and Ernestine took her writing pad from her desk and started to make notes on which paintings she would hang somewhere else or exchange for some new ones that had arrived the day before. But before she could really get into it, Mr. Fisher called her to his office, bade her to sit down on the rickety leather chair, folded his hands and showed her a piece of paper. Ernestine unfolded the piece of paper and started to read:

LAST WILL & TESTAMENT

THIS Last Will & Testament is made by me Abraham Gaylord Fisher of 34 Albemarle Street, City of Westminster, London W1S.

I REVOKE all previous wills and codicils.

I APPOINT as executors and trustees of my will JOHN M. GOULD of ROLLINGSONS CHANCERY LANE OFFICE, MARLBOROUGH COURT, 14-18 HOLBORN, LONDON EC1N 2LE and FREDERIK L. GOULD of ROLLINGSONS CHANCERY LANE OFFICE, MARLBOROUGH COURT, 14-18 HOLBORN, LONDON EC1N 2LE.

I GIVE THE GALLERY WITH ALL ITS CONTENTS to ERNESTINE SOPHIE LECLERC.

I GIVE the rest of my estate to my executors and trustees to hold in trust to pay my debts, taxes and testamentary expenses and pay the residue to ERNESTINE SOPHIE LECLERC.

There were some illegible signatures on the bottom of the page but Ernestine just sat there unable to move. Slowly she lifted her head and looked at Mr. Fisher.

"Why?" she asked.

"Because you care about the paintings ... more than anyone else I know. I have no family left and you will transform this dark place into a sophisticated specialty gallery. Something I always wanted to do but could not. At heart, I am a simple man unable to envision change. Be it in the gallery or life. I resist change with a vengeance.

So please, Ernestine, forgive me my harsh words and abrupt manners. It is all I know to protect me. I wish you a good life and once in a while remember me with kindness. Farewell Ernestine." With these words, he turned around and left the office with his short umbrella and his hat.

Ernestine heard the front door open and close and then she was alone. She sat in the office for a long while. Her thoughts went all over the place. From Jonathan and what he would have done with this legacy, to Eric, who somehow had disappeared, to Robin and his Lordship. More memories wanted to intrude but Ernestine got up quickly and walked into the gallery.

"My gallery," she thought, and a shudder shook her body. She could not identify whether it was from joy or fright. "But Mr. Fisher still has many years to live so I do not have to worry about this." She made a cup of strong black tea while cataloguing the new arrivals.

Time passed by quickly and when the daylight had to be replaced with electric lights, Ernestine put down her pad and pencil and reentered the office. She quickly glanced at the old grandfather clock standing in a dark corner and saw that it was already after four o'clock. She had a few errands to run before the stores closed, so she locked up the gallery and left. She did not hear the phone ringing.

Chapter 23
Robin's Dilemma

When she finally arrived home, exhausted and her arms full of packages and bags she saw a figure sitting on the steps. At first, she did not recognize the person but the instant she heard her name she knew it was Robin.

"What are you doing here? You should have called," she said.

"I wanted to surprise you. Let me help you with the groceries."

Ernestine gave him some bags and looked at him.

"You have changed. Your clothes are tailor-made and the fabric is just divine. Have you just come from Bond Street?" She teased him.

Robin followed her up the stairs to her apartment. They put the bags on the kitchen table and Ernestine started to put their contents in the fridge, the cupboards, and some in the bathroom. She quickly changed from her working outfit into some easy beige pants and a sea-green sweater.

When she returned to the kitchen, Robin was looking out the window to the busy street below. A light rain had started to fall and the people below were hurrying to find shelter. Before Ernestine reached the window, thunder cracked and lightning raced across the dark sky. There was an extremely loud thunderclap, the kitchen light flickered for a moment and then went out.

Ernestine grabbed a few candles from the kitchen drawer and lit them with a match. Shadows danced along the walls in slow motion and she went quickly to close all the open windows. Robin had stayed in the kitchen and Ernestine remembered that as a boy he was terrified of thunder and lightning. She hurried back and found him still by the window, petrified and his dark eyes were immense with a terror unknown to her. She had always liked the wild weather, especially thunder and lightning. She approached Robin and took his hand:

"Let's sit down here at the table and have a glass of wine." With these words she guided him to the chair and then brought out some glasses and an open bottle of red wine. She poured the wine, being careful not to spill any on Robin. He did not say a word but just sat there, still as a statue. Ernestine opened the fridge and with a candle lit its contents.

"I have all the ingredients to make some small sandwiches," she said to herself and took out the tomatoes, cucumbers, lettuce, pate, ham and cheese. She even had half an avocado left from breakfast. She arranged the delicacies on a plate and made each one of them an open sandwich.

She tried to get Robin's attention away from the weather but was unsuccessful. Luckily, after a few more minutes the electricity came back. The light overhead illuminated the whole kitchen, and the refrigerator was humming again. Ernestine looked out the window and the rain had stopped. There was still occasional lightning but in the distance. She closed the curtains and turned toward Robin.

"I am a fool, Ernestine; I have never gotten over my childhood fear of thunder and lightning."

"Don't mention it. Let's have something to eat."

They munched on their sandwiches in silence until Ernestine asked, "What brings you here?'

"I had to come to London for some business for Lord Fairfax and as I was done early I was able to get away without having to spend the evening with the lawyers. So I thought I'd come and see how you are doing."

"You have never been good at not telling me the truth. So tell me the real reason you are here."

Robin got up, went around the table to Ernestine and knelt down on one knee. Before Ernestine could say anything Robin asked her, "Will you marry me, Ernestine?"

She was taken aback and her mind filled with images from a long time ago ... she and Robin as children playing at her grandmother's house; Robin coming to San Diego; and Jonathan. Jonathan who was a part of her and the pain of having lost him rushed through her like a raging wildfire. She felt tears welling up in her eyes and she turned away.

When she had gotten her emotions somewhat under control, she said in a small voice:

"Give me some time, Robin. I did not expect this at all and I just do not know what I am feeling right now."

Robin started to say something but Ernestine cut him off. "Please Robin, leave me. I need to be alone just now."

Robin took her hands in his, kissed them and gave her a long look, then turned and without a word left the apartment.

Ernestine slumped into her chair and the tears started to flow. She did not realize how long she had been sitting there, but it was a long time. Her back hurt and her head was buzzing. Slowly she got up, went to the bathroom and washed her face and then made her way to her bedroom.

She crawled into her soft bed and tried to sleep. But sleep was elusive and she was haunted by events of her past. When she finally fell asleep, morning was breaking.

Chapter 24
Sam

When Ernestine finally woke up, the sun was already high in the sky. It was a wintry sun and the world looked like a watercolor painting where too much water was used and nothing seemed to have sharp contours. She got up, went to the kitchen, and put on the kettle for a cup of tea.

It was cold in her apartment and she returned to the bedroom to put on a thick sweater over her pajamas. Her eyes fell on an odd-sized envelope that had been pushed under the door. She picked it up and recognized Robin's handwriting. She took the letter to the kitchen and put it on the table. She did not want to read it right now. Slowly, her mind remembered yesterday evening and she started to shiver.

"What on earth am I going to do about Robin? He is a lovely man, very attractive, and one of my best friends. Is this enough to marry him? I do like him, but…"

At that moment the kettle whistled and she went to pour the boiling water into her little stainless steel teapot, the one she had received as a gift from an old friend of her mother's. Some of the water spilled over and Ernestine realized that she had to pay attention to what she was doing.

She toasted a slice of bread, got some blue cheese and strawberry jam from the fridge and sat down to eat her breakfast. Her thoughts were miles away, across the ocean and in the past.

She remembered the mornings when Jonathan would make her breakfast and they would eat together on the sunny balcony overlooking San Diego Bay. Tears started to run lazily down her cheeks like a little creek during dry summers. She listlessly munched on her toast and finally put it away. She was not hungry.

The tea was nice and hot but burned her mouth. She got up, cleared the table and took a shower. She donned gray flannel slacks and a white sweater. She pulled up her hair and wound a green-blue scarf around her neck. She grabbed her purse and coat and slipped into some sensible shoes. She locked the door and left the apartment building.

By now, the sky was overcast and a short while after light rain started to fall. She opened her red umbrella that she always carried in her purse, and hurried around the corner where she promptly bumped into someone with a black umbrella. She murmured an apology and wanted to hurry on when the stranger said, "Well Ernestine, what a way to start the weekend."

Ernestine looked up and her eyes met the dark eyes of Sam who worked at the bank where Mr. Fisher did his business.

"I apologize for walking into you," Ernestine said and wanted to hurry on; but Sam held her by her arm and asked, "Please Ernestine, join me for a cup of coffee at the pub. I am sure Mr. Fisher will be fine without you for half an hour."

Ernestine looked up at him and saw an impish smile playing around his mouth. His eyes shone with a friendly smile and Ernestine had to laugh. "Okay, I guess it will be alright with Mr. Fisher."

They entered the pub, ordered coffee and scones, and talked about this and that. Soon the half hour was gone. They paid, got up and walked to the door. Outside, Sam said, "This was too short to get to know you a bit. What do you say we continue the conversation after work here?"

"Sounds good to me," said Ernestine. "See you around five o'clock."

They each opened the umbrella and walked in opposite directions. When Ernestine arrived at the gallery she found Mr. Fisher busy with a customer. She went to the back room to finish up with some paperwork. Her thoughts jumped from work to Sam and she had a curious feeling that she could not quite put her finger on.

The day was uneventful and she found herself checking the big clock more often than usual. The hands did not seem to move at all. But finally, it was time to close the gallery and Ernestine bade Mr. Fisher a good weekend and hurried out into the street.

When she got close to the pub she thought, "What if Sam is not there?" But she pushed the thought away and entered the pub. To her great relief, Sam was sitting at a small window table with a beer in front of him. Ernestine joined him with an orange juice and they continued their conversation.

A couple of hours later Sam invited her to dinner at a little diner close by. Ernestine accepted and they walked across the street to find the little local. It only had a few tables with checkered tablecloths and matching napkins. It was warm and cozy and they sat down at a table close to the fireplace.

They ordered Shepherd's pie with all the trimmings. The food was good and plentiful. They ate in silence, each lost in their own thoughts. When they had finished, Sam took her arm and they walked out into the night. It had started to rain again and it was cold.

"Sam," Ernestine said, "I live just around the corner. I can make some tea, coffee or whatever else you'd like and we do not have to stand in the cold."

"Okay," Sam answered.

They quickly arrived at her front door and climbed the stairs to her apartment. While Ernestine tried to find the keys, Sam looked at her pensively.

"Why do you look at me that way? Ah, here are the keys," and Ernestine opened the door and entered her home. She took off her shoes and raincoat, showed Sam to the living room, and quickly went to change from her office clothes to something more comfortable like her old blue jeans and the green sweatshirt.

"Would you like some tea or coffee?" she asked Sam.

"Tea would be just perfect."

Ernestine went to the kitchen to put on the kettle when she felt Sam's arms around her. He slowly turned her toward him and kissed her lightly on her lips. Ernestine felt instantly weak and had to lean against him. He gently guided her toward her bedroom where he softly sat her down.

Ernestine looked at him and felt a wave of emotions sweep over her. She was glad she was sitting as she could feel her knees wobbling. Sam embraced her and tenderly pushed her into the pillows. He took off her sweatshirt and caressed her bare arms so gently that Ernestine shivered under his touch.

Sam looked at her intently to find out how she liked to be touched. Had he asked her, she would have been unable to tell him. He realized very quickly that her inner forearms and hands were her weak spots and teased feelings out of her that she had almost forgotten.

They brought memories back of Jonathan and the way he would make love to her. This memory brought tears to her eyes and they slowly rolled down her cheeks. Sam did not ask any questions but softly kissed the tears away while stroking her neck and playing with her hair.

Ernestine wanted him to stop, but not really. She was torn between what she thought she should do and what her body wanted so badly. Sam seemed to understand the inner turmoil and kissed her lips and whispered, "Enjoy it, Ernestine. This is for you. I have watched you for many weeks and realized that you carry a deep sorrow within you. Let me alleviate it for tonight and make you feel beautiful."

Ernestine could only look at him and wonder that he found her attractive. Sam was just slightly taller than

Ernestine with black, soft hair and dark expressive eyes. His mouth was beautifully curved and ready to be kissed. He was very muscular and not a hint of fat on him. His skin was soft and warm, and Ernestine luxuriated in his embrace.

"Enjoy," he whispered as he continued to caress her. As her body started to wake to his touch he carefully removed her kami and bra and continued to explore every part of her. His lips brushed against her nipples which instantly grew hard and sent a signal to other parts of her body making it impossible for her to stop him.

When he saw that she was no longer rational and that her emotional needs had taken over, he slowly pulled off her jeans and panties and touched her legs, feet, and knees until he finally came close to her most vulnerable part. But he did not touch it. Ernestine was moving with his caresses trying to bring herself to his hands. Finally, she could no longer bear it and whispered, "Please Sam, release me."

Sam took her into his arms, touched her most sensitive part and watched her as the waves of pleasure washed over her transporting her into a realm heretofore unknown to her.

Ernestine shuddered and Sam held her close. Only now did she realize that he was still wearing his clothes, adding to her feeling of vulnerability. She looked at him and started to open the buttons of his shirt. When he did not object she continued undressing him. It was a new discovery for her to undress a man.

When she was done and his clothes were on the floor, she looked at him, took his hand and licked his wrist. He sighed and let her do whatever she wanted. It was now Ernestine's turn to explore. She touched, kissed and caressed his gorgeous body until he could no longer take it.

Ernestine quickly straddled him and guided him inside her. With slow movements she brought him to climax and enjoyed his release as much as hers. She watched him being in his own pleasure world; and when he was spent they clung together in silence. After a while Sam said, "I should go and let you sleep."

"Please stay until the morning, Sam; I would like to wake up in your arms."

So Sam stayed until the early morning. They made love again but then Sam had to leave.

Ernestine stayed in the warm bed. So many unwanted thoughts were invading her mind and sleep was long in coming.

Chapter 25
A Strange Phone Call

Ernestine was awakened by the shrill telephone ringing five minutes after she had finally fallen into an uneasy slumber. She reached over to grab the receiver on her nightstand and sleepily answered the phone. At the other end, an unknown voice told her to come back to San Diego as quickly as possible. Ernestine thought she was dreaming but eventually realized that it was Mr. Connor who was calling.

"What is wrong, Mr. Connor?" a sleepy-voiced Ernestine asked.

"Please, do come home with the earliest plane possible. I will be at the airport as soon as you let me know your arrival time. I can also drive up to L.A. if that makes it easier for you."

"But why is it urgent that I come back?"

"I cannot tell you over the phone. Please Mrs. Leclerc, believe me you need to be here and want to be here."

"I don't have any wish right now to come back to California, so whatever this is it will have to wait. If it is something with the rental, please call the property manager and they can take care of it." Good-bye, Mr. Connor.

Ernestine angrily slammed the receiver onto the phone. She began to think about this strange phone call and was about to dial her lawyers when the phone rang again. It was Father Carroll.

"Hi, Ernestine." His friendly voice boomed through the airspace. "Sorry to wake you so early in the morning, but a very upset Mr. Connor just called me asking that I talk to you and make you come back immediately. I know, my dear, this is a very strange request; but believe me, it is imperative that you come as soon as possible. A life hangs in the balance. However, I cannot tell you more than this.

Please believe me when I tell you that you have to come. Let me know when you arrive and we will have a car at the airport ready for you."

"But why is it such a mystery?"

"Listen, we do not have much time. I took the liberty and booked you on Air New Zealand flight 0001, leaving Heathrow at 4:15 pm and arriving at LAX at 7:45 pm. Please, Ernestine, take that plane. See you soon."

With these words, Father Carroll hung up and Ernestine stood incredulously in the middle of the room with the dead receiver beeping in her hands.

A quick look at the old clock on the wall told her that she had to get moving if she wanted to catch that flight. She quickly showered, called the gallery to let Mr. Fisher know that she had to return to San Diego due to an emergency and would let him know when she would be back.

She cut his questions short telling him that she had to leave for the airport in a couple of hours and would tell him all about it on her return. She hung up and started to pack a few things.

She preferred not to think about the strange call, but decided that if Father Carroll was involved it must be something serious. She called a taxi service and was picked up at the apartment within the hour.

Traffic was not too bad and soon she was dropped off at Heathrow Airport. Check-in was quick and efficient and Ernestine proceeded to the lounge to wait for boarding. When her flight was called she walked to the gate and boarded the plane.

Once she was seated, she allowed her mind to go to the events of the past few days. Mr. Fisher's will, Robin's proposal, the night with Sam, and now the mysterious phone call from Father Carroll that made her drop everything and hop on a plane.

Curiosity is an incredibly strong motivator and Ernestine found herself speculating what the emergency might be. For one, Mr. Connor was involved; otherwise, why would he have called her first? Then Father Carroll. It must be important for that busy man to take the time and call her and have someone make the reservation for her.

There were not that many people that knew Ernestine, Mr. Connor and Father Carroll. One name popped into her head: Mary-Ann. Did something happen to her? Ernestine realized that she had not thought about Mary-Ann in a very long time and she could not imagine that Mary-Ann would try to contact her, even less through Father Carroll.

There were other acquaintances of both women who had both their addresses. Ernestine concluded that it could not be Mary-Ann. Could something have happened with a rental home? But again, that would be handled by the property management company and they would have contacted her should her presence be required.

Ernestine found herself at a loss and was glad when the flight attendant offered her some orange juice before take-off. Once in the air, Ernestine accommodated herself in her seat, took the book she had grabbed from her bag, and started to read.

Dinner was served a couple of hours after take-off and thereafter Ernestine tried to sleep. Air travel always made her sleepy and so she closed her eyes and dozed off. When she woke up from her slumber, it was still daylight and it took her a moment to put her thoughts in order.

She asked for a glass of water and watched the movie that was playing on her screen. She had no idea what it was all about and turned it off. A few hours later and halfway through her book, it was announced that that they would be landing at LAX on time. Ernestine was wondering who would be picking her up but decided that whoever it was would probably not know what this whole trip was all about. She would have to wait until she met with Father Carroll and Mr. Connor. After an uneventful flight, they finally landed at LAX.

Ernestine gathered her bag and proceeded to immigration and customs. When she approached the arrival hall, she saw Father Carroll and Mr. Connor waiting for her. Her heart sank, and she had an ominous feeling that something was terribly wrong.

She walked hastily toward them and hugged both men.

"You look splendid," said Father Carroll approvingly. "London seems to agree with you."

"It's a fun town and I have always liked it. It brings back memories of my childhood, the visits to London with my parents or my grandparents, the lush parks, and of course a ride on the tube," replied Ernestine.

While walking to the parking structure to retrieve their car, Father Carroll began telling her what had happened recently and the reason for his urgent phone call to her early in the morning.

"It all started with a call from the law offices where the late Kevin Masters had worked. As far as I can gather, Eric Massy is a patient at the Scripps La Jolla Hospital where Mary-Ann used to work. He was badly hurt in some kind of an accident abroad; and when he was finally able to be moved was brought to San Diego."

"What happened!" exclaimed Ernestine with a worried look on her face.

"We do not know," answered Father Carroll. "It seems that someone told the hospital abroad that they should take him to San Diego. So they had a medical transport arranged and brought him here. The company he worked for is paying for everything as the accident happened during one of his trips abroad. As far as Ron and I could gather there was some explosion at an oil well somewhere in Africa and several people were killed and some badly injured. I guess Eric is lucky to be alive. Anyhow, that is all we know. We will stop at the hospital on our way back to San Diego, and if you feel up to it you may be able to visit with Eric for a few minutes."

Ernestine sat very still absorbing the disturbing news. She had not thought of Eric in quite awhile. Being in London had removed her physically from all that had been her life on the west coast. Hearing Father Carroll's words opened the floodgates in her mind; and like wild water, memories came rushing in. All of a sudden she felt extremely tired and empty. She did not want to deal with her past right now, but understood that it had to be done.

The drive continued in silence until the car stopped in front of the hospital. Father Joe helped her out of the car and guided her inside to the information desk. A friendly older man was manning the post, and when Father Joe had stated his business, the man quickly called a nurse who took charge of them.

She escorted them to an impressive oak door with a beautiful brass handle and after a short knock she showed them in. The woman behind the desk was in her late fifties and looked very efficient. She wore a gray suit that highlighted her skillfully-coiffed unusual white hair. An air of competence radiated from her and Ernestine immediately felt at ease.

"Please sit down," she said, and pointed to a cozy sitting area in the corner of her office. "My name is Emilia and I am in charge of the hospital. You must be Ernestine," she stated with a soft voice and sat down opposite Ernestine on a large sofa chair.

Ernestine nodded. She bent her head and studied her hands. The soft voice continued:

"About three months ago we received a request from a large company to accommodate an employee of theirs that had been hurt in an oil well blow-out in Africa. He was badly burned in the accident and had broken his left leg in several places where an iron beam had pinned him to the ground making it impossible for him to escape. That is all we know about the accident.

"However, we made all the necessary arrangements and had the patient flown in as soon as it was possible to move him. Our staff assessed the damage he had sustained and started with the operations. He was kept in an artificial coma for some time. A few weeks ago, it was decided to bring him out of the coma and evaluate possible brain damage.

"To our surprise, his brainwaves were normal. He is a very lucky fellow. Anyhow, he did not have any visitors and the company did not know of any close relatives or friends, so he stayed here and the nurses and doctors took turns visiting him more often than was required. Mind you, he was under heavy sedation and talking to him was and is still not possible.

"However, the nurses heard him say one word over and over again: Ernestine. We concluded that this must be his wife, his friend, his child, a relative or somebody close to him. But we were unsuccessful in ascertaining who this person is until one day a nurse told us that a doctor who had worked here some time ago had a friend called Ernestine. And that this Ernestine had also been a patient here.

"We researched the archives and found that Mary-Ann Masters had a patient called Ernestine. Her address was in our files and we tried to contact her by phone and by letter. Nothing happened; and then we received a phone call from Mr. Connor. Mary-Ann had gotten our messages and tried to call you for permission to give us your address. However, she was unsuccessful.

"She then called your property management company to find out your whereabouts, but they said they did not know either. One of the employees remembered that you had helped a family and they found Mr. Connor. He was contacted by the property management company as they thought he could get a hold of you and get your permission to release the information. As he did not know exactly where you were, they left it at that.

"However, he went to see Father Carroll who then in turn went to talk to the property management company explaining the circumstances and obtained your contact phone number. We thought it best that either Mr. Connor or Father Joe contact you. And so finally here you are. I will take you to his room if you feel up to it."

Ernestine looked up into the gentle face and whispered, "Yes."

They all got up and went down a long corridor. At the end was a door with a small sign on it that said: "Please No Visitors."

"We had to make sure that Eric would not be disturbed by lost patients or visitors. His situation was extremely critical. He is stable now, but needs all the rest he can get. Sometimes, he opens his eyes for a few moments but he does not seem to see anything. He can only speak a few words and does not seem to know where he is."

She opened the door and let Ernestine enter.

"Father Carroll and I will be right here if you need us." And with these words she closed the door behind Ernestine.

Ernestine took one more step toward the bed, adjusting her eyes to the semi-darkness. She could hardly make out a person in the bed but when she got closer she saw that there was a human being lying in the bed. The head was heavily bandaged and only a little of the face was visible. A cage with taut wires held up the left leg at an angle and the left arm was in a cast. Ernestine approached the bed cautiously and took the right hand into her hands. She looked intently at the little she could see of his handsome face, but there was no movement at all.

"Eric," she whispered. "It is me, Ernestine."

Slowly, ever so slowly, Eric opened his eyes and tried to focus, his lips started to tremble, but no sound could be heard. All of a sudden, Ernestine felt the hand she was holding in hers moving and she slightly pressed it. Eric tried to move his head but it was too much.

"Be still, Eric," Ernestine spoke softly. "I will stay here until the nurse tells me to leave." She had hardly spoken the last word when the door opened and Emilia waved to her to come. Ernestine got up and kissed Eric gently on his cheek. A shudder went through him and then he said in a small voice, "Ernestine?"

"I am here Eric. Sleep now and when you wake up I will be here again."

With these words she turned and slowly walked to the door where she collapsed into Father Carroll's arms.

They went back to Emilia's office and Ernestine sat shocked on the dark brown sofa.

Emilia told her that Eric was getting better but very slowly and that only time could tell whether he would ever fully recover from his grave injuries. The doctors had agreed to let Ernestine come and be with him to see if that would give him the will to fight. Without it, he would most probably remain in this semiconscious state. His bones will eventually heal but his mind might be trapped.

"But," said Ernestine, "how will my being here change anything?"

"You see, the nurses and doctors that attend to Eric concluded that only a counter-shock could help him. Finally, they figured that this Ernestine, you, must be someone he deeply cares for but has lost somehow and needs to find again. So in his mind he is searching for you. By bringing you here to be with him we hope that he will realize that you are here physically in the present and that might be enough to end his mind's search. Seeing you by his bed, hearing your voice, and above all, you holding his hand, a physical contact … that may hopefully be enough to make him want to live again."

"Tell me what time I should come back tomorrow. I need to get some sleep. It's been a very long and eventful day."

"You can come anytime you want. I will leave word at the reception that you are to be allowed to visit Eric anytime."

The three of them got up, shook hands; and Father Carroll and Ernestine left the office and walked down the long corridor. Without a word, they got into the car and Mr. Connor drove off toward Ernestine's apartment.

A soft touch and a faraway voice brought Ernestine back to reality. The car was stopped at the entrance to the Harbor Club and Father Joe handed Ernestine the keys.

"We picked them up at the property management office this morning. We figured that you might want to stay at your place," he said.

Ernestine thanked him and left the two men standing by the car while she took her suitcase and disappeared through the glass doors.

"Do you think that she will visit him regularly? It is all the same an imposition on her and her time. Do you know why she left for London?" asked Mr. Connor.

"No, I certainly don't. I guess we will have to wait until she is ready to tell us. I only hope that the doctors are right and that she will make a difference in Eric's psyche."

Chapter 26
A Visit to the Hospital

With trembling hands, Ernestine opened the door to her apartment. It seemed ages since she had been here last. And yet, everything seemed to be so normal. Just like coming home from a trip abroad, ... tired yet looking forward to a long hot shower.

She kicked off her shoes, put the suitcase in the spare room and went to the balcony. She opened the large sliding door and breathed in the fresh cool air.

In her mind's eye she saw Jonathan sitting at the table together with her parents talking about the week's events. It had been a tiring week for her dad and husband and Saturday was a welcome respite from the intense work at the office.

Her Mom had suggested a little get together to refresh the tired men. They had enjoyed a light lunch and were watching the sunset over Point Loma before going out for dinner at the Top of the Market. It was an easy and pleasant walk from the apartment.

Ernestine remembered the laughter at dinner, the secret touches and the walk back. Her parents had left, and she and Jonathan could hardly wait to get out on the private balcony for some quick lovemaking.

With a sigh, Ernestine turned around and stared at the dark windows. She went inside and lit a few candles on the mantelpiece. She could not bring herself to go to the bedroom even though she was exhausted. The flight from London had been long, and seeing Eric in such a state had affected her deeply. She sat down on the soft sofa and promptly fell asleep.

The sun was high in the sky when Ernestine finally woke up. It took her a few moments to realize where she was and then she scolded herself for having slept on the sofa. But she felt refreshed all the same and took a long, hot shower. Wrapped in her favorite towel, she looked through her wardrobe and selected a pair of dark raisin-colored jeans and an off-white blouse. To make the outfit complete, she donned a dark cardigan and dark sandals.

With her sunglasses on her head, she descended to the parking garage where her car was patiently waiting. She got in and drove to the hospital. She had no idea what she expected but somehow she knew she had to go. She easily found the floor where Eric's room was located and asked at the nurses' station if it was okay for her to go and see him. The nurse on duty looked at her and nodded briefly. Ernestine walked down the corridor and hesitated a moment before knocking on the door and entering.

Eric was sleeping; at least it seemed to her that he was sleeping. His eyes were closed and he lay very still. She approached the bed, took his hand and sat down on the chair beside his bed. She silently watched him for a very long time. The silence in the room and her fatigue made her fall asleep. She awakened with a start when she felt her hand being squeezed. She opened her eyes and saw Eric looking at her. A faint smile played around his mouth as he tried to speak.

"Ernestine? Is it really you?" he whispered. "How did you find me? And where am I?"

"You are at the Scripps La Jolla Hospital." And Ernestine recounted what she had been told by Emilia and Father Carroll. Eric lay still and was silent for many minutes. Ernestine could see that his mind was wandering, trying to understand what had happened and how he got to La Jolla.

She looked at him and felt a tenderness engulf her that she had never experienced before, not even with Jonathan. She was about to break the silence when the nurse came into the room and motioned her to wait outside. Ernestine got up and turned toward the door when Eric faintly said, "Ernestine, don't go."

"I'll come back as soon as the nurse has finished."

She quickly left the room and went to the coffee machine where she ran into Emilia.

"Hi, Ernestine; it's good to see you. You look lots better than yesterday."

"I had a long sleep and that took some of the tiredness away. Any news about Eric's situation?"

"We are all hopeful that your being here will make the difference we are waiting for. Give him some time and us, so we can assess your impact on his emotional being."

"Thanks Emilia."

With her coffee cup in hand, Ernestine walked back to Eric's room where the nurse was just leaving and resumed her place at his side with his hand in hers. They remained like this for quite some time, like a picture painted by a soulful painter. Ernestine sipped her coffee and Eric had his eyes closed. Once in a while he gently pressed her hand to make sure she was still there.

When he opened his eyes again, they were full of wonder. However, his face retained little of the eternal boyish look she remembered so well. There were also unmistakable etchings of hardness and cynicism.

Ernestine wondered what had wrought this change and decided that one day she would find out. Now was neither the time nor the place. The most important thing at the moment was for Eric to get well again and to be able to leave the hospital on his own two feet.

Around 5.30 pm, the nurse brought dinner for Eric and Ernestine kept him company. She helped him eat when he needed it and held the glass for him to drink. When the dishes were cleared away Ernestine got up and said good-bye to Eric:

"I will come back tomorrow. Sleep well and sweet dreams." With these words, she gently kissed him on the mouth and left.

She drove straight back to her apartment, parked the car in the garage, and took the elevator to her floor. Again, with trembling hands she put the key in the lock and opened the door. Silence greeted her and tears started to roll down her cheeks. Memories of happy times flooded her mind and she was powerless to stop the emotions pulsating through her.

She closed the door, went to the refrigerator and poured herself a glass of white wine. With the long-stemmed glass in her hand she went out on the balcony, sat down on one of the soft chairs and gazed over the dispassionate and ageless ocean stretching out before her as infinite as human sorrow.

After a while her tears stopped, her mind calmed, and her pounding heart found its normal rhythm. For the first time she was able to think of Jonathan without feeling intense pain. There was still a longing for the way things had been but she now understood that his death offered her a new beginning. She was determined to take the opportunity and avoid loneliness and unhappiness.

Early the next morning, she drove back to the hospital where Emilia greeted her at the door.

"You look content and determined this morning. Have you made any decisions?"

"Yes, I finally figured that it is my responsibility to make myself happy, nobody else's, and I have decided to stay here and make sure that Eric will heal and be able to leave the hospital a healthy man. If my presence here is helping then that is what I will do."

Emilia took Ernestine's hands in hers and said:

"Thank you. With you here, the doctors think that he will have a speedy recovery. Maybe some broken bones will take a while, but his emotional health will improve quickly. In our estimation, you give him the reason he needs to want to live again."

Ernestine nodded and the two women walked toward Eric's room. Ernestine knocked on the door and entered. She found Eric looking out the window. When he heard the door open he slowly turned his head away from the window and focused his gaze on Ernestine. The beginning of a smile tipped the corners of his mouth and he lifted one hand to motion her to come to him.

Ernestine advanced to the bed and took his hand, looked into his eyes where a fleeting spark flickered in his deep brown eyes. He tried to speak but the words were stuck in his throat. He looked miserably at Ernestine who gently stroked his thin hands and said:

"Be quiet my love; I will stay with you as long as you want me to."

Eric exhaled a long sigh of contentment and his eyes shone with a newly-found purpose in life. Ernestine stayed most of the day at his bedside, sometimes talking to him, often just watching him sleep. As the days went by, Ernestine felt peaceful and no shadows frightened her heart.

They had fallen into a comfortable routine. Ernestine would arrive shortly after breakfast and sit with him during lunch. Sometimes she would stay until dinner time and sometimes she would leave right after lunch to run some errands. Her life took on a pattern of comfort and joy and she avoided thinking about the day when Eric would be well enough to leave the hospital and her comfortable make-believe world would tumble down in ruins.

One evening, when she returned home from the hospital, she found a letter from John M. Gould of Rollingsons Chancery Lane Office, Holborn among her mail. A wave of apprehension swept through her while she impatiently opened the letter. An official-looking document fell out of the envelope; and when she picked it up she realized that it was a death certificate issued for Abraham Gaylord Fisher.

A suffocating sensation tightened her throat and the paper fell to the floor. On unsteady legs she walked to the sofa and sank down to read the letter in its entirety. It said that Mr. Fisher had died of cancer and his remains had been cremated at the City of London Cemetery. And the ashes scattered in the Garden of Rest.

A flash of devastating grief ripped through her as she remembered his kindly face that she now would never behold again. With trembling hands she took out the rest of the sheets and read through them. John Gould kindly requested she come to London to take care of the legalities of her inheritance. He reckoned that a fortnight would be enough to clear everything and hand over the gallery and other objects.

Ernestine was stunned beyond belief. Somehow she had not quite believed the she would actually inherit Mr. Fisher's gallery. It had seemed to her just a whim of the older gentleman. Faced with the prospect of owning a gallery in London while trying to help Eric made her intensely aware of the fact that she was quite alone in the world.

She had no friends left in San Diego and she did not want to contact anyone at Jonathan's law firm. In her wretchedness she decided to call Mr. Connor. He answered the phone at the second ring and patiently listened to Ernestine. When she had finished, he suggested that she might want to call Robin in London to let him know she was coming and to arrange an appointment with the lawyers. As for him, he would pick her up whenever she needed and drive her to the airport.

Relieved, Ernestine put down the receiver and checked available flights to London. She would leave the day after tomorrow. This would give her time to see Eric and tell him that she would be gone for a couple of weeks. Now that she knew what she had to do, she enjoyed the prospect of going back to London. She booked herself a ticket on British Airways, leaving in the evening and arriving at Heathrow the next afternoon.

She called Robin and asked if he could make the arrangements with the lawyers. She gave him her flight itinerary and he promised to pick her up at the airport. She quickly called Mr. Connor and told him that she would take a cab to the airport the following day.

With her travel arrangements done she went out on the balcony and caught the last rays of the setting sun before they disappeared into the vast ocean. She looked silently at the rising harvest moon and wondered where all the souls of the dead would gather tonight.

Chapter 27
The Man in the Wheelchair

The next day when Ernestine arrived at the hospital, she was greeted by a smiling Emilia, and Eric in a wheelchair beside her. He held out his hand and Ernestine took it gently, trying in vain to suppress the tears that filled her eyes.

"Oh Eric, you are making such rapid progress that soon you will leave this hospital." She did not add … "and no longer need me and leave me."

"It is all thanks to you Ernestine. Without you here I would not have healed so quickly," he replied and took Ernestine's hand. He looked up at her and asked shyly:

"Will you take me out into the open so I can breathe fresh air and look at the world with new eyes?"

"Of course; let's go."

Emilia held the door open for them and Ernestine pushed the wheelchair outside. The weather was as usual perfect. The sky had that particular hue of blue only found in Southern California; the wind gently brushed the leaves of the ornamental trees and a few leaves that had completed their life cycle slowly glided to the floor in a harmonious dance. The sun had already warmed the square pavers and the heat radiated from them. Eric sighed and touched Ernestine's hand that was pushing the wheelchair:

"Soon, Ernestine, I will get out of this contraption and you and I will walk these grounds together. The doctors have high hopes that I will be able to do so before Thanksgiving."

"That is great news, and I am looking forward to walking with you again. However, I will not be able to come and see you for a couple of weeks. I have to go back to London and take care of some business. But I also hope to be back before Thanksgiving."

Ernestine could not see the dark cloud that passed over Eric's face and the pain that filled his beautiful eyes. However, when he spoke, his voice sounded the same as before and Ernestine thought that it did not seem to matter to him whether she was here or not.

"Promise me, Ernestine, that you do not stay too long over there and come and see me as soon as you get back."

"Of course I will come and see you as soon as I am back. I booked the flight for tomorrow afternoon and as I said I hope to be back before Thanksgiving. I will tell you all about my London stay on my return. I am afraid it is quite a long and winding road."

"Looking forward to that," Eric replied.

They fell silent and Ernestine pushed the wheelchair toward a bench, and sat down. They both looked out over the blue water, both deep in thoughts. After a while, Ernestine got up energetically, looked at Eric, and said:

"Promise me you will not disappear from the hospital while I am in England."

"I promise," Eric said with a boyish twinkle in his eyes.

"Good; then that is settled, and the moment I am back I will come to the hospital."

Ernestine took Eric back to his room where the nurses helped him into bed. She kissed him lightly on the cheek and bid him a good time. She quickly turned and left the room. In the corridor outside she briefly talked with Emilia who confirmed that Eric would not be discharged before Thanksgiving.

Ernestine drove back to her apartment and started to pack a few things. She realized that she still had clothes at the apartment in London and wondered what she was going to do with them and the furniture.

"Maybe I should just give it all away and start fresh here. But what if Eric's plans do not include me?" The thought made her shiver and she realized how much this man meant to her. Ever since he had picked her up, frail and sick, from the same hospital he was staying at now, he had been an important part of her life. He was like the anchor that prevented her from being swept away by life's ups and downs.

He had given her enough space to find herself again when she was lost in a maelstrom of emotions after Jonathan's accident, provided her with a safe haven, and had been there for her when she needed companionship. It was she who had run out after Tara's accusations without leaving word where she was going. Without Father Carroll's phone call she might never have seen him again. She vowed that this was not going to happen again.

Ernestine resolutely went to the kitchen for a glass of water and took it out onto the balcony. She sat down in one of the soft lounge chairs and started to quickly write down the things she had to take care of in London. There was of course the gallery that needed her attention, the flat had to be vacated and its contents disposed of, she needed to talk to Lord Fairfax and Robin, the bank accounts had to be arranged, and then there was Sam.

Ernestine wondered whether she should try to see him one more time and decided to leave this to the last minute. Time has a way of sorting these things out. She got up and looked out over the deep blue water, went inside to the kitchen and made herself an open sandwich with the 12-grain bread that she and Jonathan liked so much for their sandwiches, put some lettuce on it, slices of vine-ripened tomatoes, avocado from Fallbrook, a thick slice of provolone cheese and some Black Forest ham.

She took her plate to the living room and slumped down on the sofa and turned on the television set. She watched the news while eating but turned it off as soon as she was done eating. She took the dishes to the kitchen and quickly washed them in the sink and put them away. She did not like to leave the dishwasher with dirty dishes while she was away. She then went to her bedroom and finished packing. She closed the suitcase and put it in the hallway, she took a warm bath in the custom-made Jacuzzi tub and went to bed for an early night.

Ernestine was asleep almost instantly and when the alarm clock played its awakening tune, it seemed to her as if she had only just fallen asleep. She did not remember having dreamed anything. She crawled out of bed, made herself breakfast, ate it on the balcony, and then stepped into the shower for a cool wash. Refreshed, she donned a pair of dark gray DNKY jeans, a light gray sweater and put a colorful scarf around her neck that highlighted her red hair beautifully.

She called a cab to pick her up in an hour, tidied the apartment, put on her travelling shoes, and was ready by the time the intercom rang and the doorman told her that her cab was waiting for her. She grabbed her coat, purse and suitcase, locked the door behind her, and took the elevator to the lobby.

The doorman helped her with the luggage and wished her a safe flight. It only took fifteen minutes to get to the airport where the cab driver checked in the luggage for her and handed her the tags. Ernestine walked to security and ordered a coffee in the little coffee shop after the security check. Soon her flight was called and she boarded the big and shiny British Airways plane that would take her to Heathrow.

Chapter 28
Back in London

After many hours, the plane safely landed and Ernestine gathered her belongings and proceeded to immigration and customs. Luckily, there were few flights arriving and she was outside within 40 minutes. She looked around and spotted Robin standing by a vending machine.

He turned and his face lit up when he saw her. He came toward her and gave her a big hug and a big kiss on her cheek. For anybody watching them it looked as if the brother had come to pick up his sister from a trip. Together they left the airport and drove to the city. They spoke little and Ernestine was thankful for the silence.

She did not know how to tell Robin that she had spent most of her time in San Diego visiting Eric at a hospital. She felt like a coward but knew that rather sooner than later she had to tell him. As if Robin had been reading her thoughts he asked:

"Whatever was it that made you go back to San Diego in such a hurry, without telling anyone about it?"

In this instant, Ernestine decided to tell him. She owed him that much.

"I received a phone call from Father Carroll that a friend of mine and Jonathan's was in a bad way in a hospital in San Diego and that he had been asking for me. The doctors did not give him much of a chance and thought that having me visiting him might give him the will to live again."

Ernestine could feel Robin's eyes on her but continued her story without looking at him.

"I visited him every day and over the weeks he has improved so much that actually yesterday he was in a wheelchair for the first time and I could take him outside. I promised him I would come back as soon as my affairs here are in order, hopefully before Thanksgiving."

"You will not stay in London then?" asked Robin in a strangled voice.

"No, I will go back. I have lost this man once before and I do not want to lose him again."

Ernestine hated herself for being so cruel to Robin but there was no kind or gentle way to tell him that she would never be his wife. During the long flight, Ernestine had forced herself to look at her life and figure out what she wanted. To her amazement, she realized that Eric meant more to her than any other living being and that she wanted desperately to stay with him.

She acknowledged to herself that it may not happen that way. Eric could be married, have a girlfriend or just not be interested in her anymore. But she had to take that risk. She had to find out. She could not face a life without knowing this and always wonder what if....

Robin had turned off the motorway and pulled into a small inn by the road. Ernestine looked at him puzzled but before she could say anything a young woman came toward Robin and kissed him on the cheek. Ernestine got out of the car and Robin introduced the young woman to her:

"This is Anette, the daughter of a friend of my father's."

The young woman came around the car and gave Ernestine a hug and said:

"Robin has told me so much about you and I am really pleased to meet you."

Anette was slightly shorter than Robin with thick curly brown hair, fair skin with a few freckles and large expressive brown eyes. Her mouth was small with lips ready for a kiss.

"Nice to meet you too," Ernestine replied. Anette reminded her of somebody but she could not think of whom right now. She was wondering what the relationship between Robin and Anette was. Were they just acquaintances due to their fathers being friends? But then why would Robin talk to her about her? Her thoughts were interrupted when Robin suggested to go into the inn and have some lunch.

They were seated by the window overlooking a typical English garden. The summer flowers had faded long ago and most of the leaves had already fallen to the ground. The world is getting ready for quiet time, thought Ernestine. They ordered a light lunch and Anette asked her:

"Are you coming to the Manor on the weekend? We have a dinner party and dancing afterward to celebrate my parents' anniversary. We would be delighted to have you."

I do not think so, Anette" Ernestine replied, "I have business to attend to here in London and as soon as all is sorted out I need to go back to the States. But thank you anyway for the invitation."

Anette turned to Robin and said, "You are coming, aren't you?"

Yes, I promised my father I would accompany him and make sure he does not get into any mischief."

They laughed just as lunch was served. Ernestine liked Anette's easy manner and felt very comfortable around her. During lunch she observed Robin and Anette and decided that Anette liked Robin very much and that also Robin was attracted to her.

Presently, Robin told her that Anette had lived in Boston for a few years and been in charge of a small gallery on Charles Street in Bacon Hill. She had come back to England after her divorce and had lived with her parents at times or in her London flat. They only met a short time ago at a fundraising function for the village. Since then, they had met occasionally whenever both happened to be in London at the same time.

"Anette called me this morning saying that she was in London so we decided to meet here for lunch," said Robin.

"I am happy to have met you Anette," said Ernestine, "and I hope I will see more of you in London, time permitting."

They chatted for a little while longer and then Robin suggested to head for the city and take Ernestine to her flat.

"I assume you would like to take a shower or a nap, before we go out for dinner?"

"Thanks Robin, but more than anything I need to sleep. We can have dinner tomorrow night if you both are still in the city?"

"Let's do that," chimed Anette, not in the least sad that she would be deprived of Ernestine's company this evening.

They dropped her off at the flat and Robin helped her with the luggage. On the way up he asked, "How do you like her?"

"She is a lovely woman from the short time I have spent with you both and I think that she does like you a lot."

"I like her too," he answered absentmindedly, and then realized that he had said it to Ernestine.

Ernestine saw the embarrassment on his face and she had to laugh out loud.

"Oh Robin, we have been friends for such a long time. Nothing and nobody will ever change that."

He put her luggage down and she hugged him and kissed him on the cheek.

"Call me tomorrow when you are up. I am here and available to you. We have an appointment with the lawyers tomorrow afternoon at two o'clock. Pick you up at noon so we can have some lunch. You do not want to go to a meeting with lawyers on an empty stomach."

With these words, Robin turned around and sauntered down the stairs.

Ernestine looked around her flat and it felt as if she had just stepped into another world. She had the eerie feeling that she had just come home from a day's work at the gallery. The weeks she had spent in San Diego seem to have disappeared like dreams in the morning when they fade gradually from your mind until only faint feelings remain.

Out of habit, she went to the fridge to get a glass of water. She opened the door and to her surprise, the fridge was stocked with all types of foods, drinks, water, even a bottle of her favorite wine was there. She smiled. Robin is really my best friend. I hope that he and Anette will find their way together and be happy ever after.

Ernestine carried her suitcase to the bedroom, unpacked, found a pajama in the dresser drawer and went to bed. Sleep was kind and came quickly. Bad dreams stayed away and she had a long and restful night. When the morning sun peeked through the curtains and kissed her cheek she woke up fully refreshed and ready to take on the day. She dressed carefully, elegant but not outlandish, put on a touch of make-up and called Robin. He answered after the first ring.

"Have you been sitting on the phone?" Ernestine teased him.

"I have done nothing all morning but waiting for this thing to ring," he replied with a happy undertone in his voice.

A short time later Ernestine and Robin were on their way to meet with John and Frederic Gould, the executors of Mr. Fisher's will. Soon they arrived at the old building in Holborn. Ernestine was nervous and Robin took her hand.

"It reminds me of the meeting with Jonathan's lawyers," Ernestine whispered, and her eyes filled with tears. Ever so gently Robin wiped them off her cheeks with a Kleenex and whispered back:

"Just think of the time we were called before your grandparents because we had quarreled and they wanted us to be friends again."

Ernestine remembered the incident and a shy smile flitted across her face.

"Thanks Robin, I needed that."

They entered through wooden doors and were guided upstairs where they were asked to wait. Almost immediately, a huge wooden door opened and Mr. John Gould motioned them inside.

"Mrs. Leclerc, I assume," he said, "and…."

"Robin Fairfax," Robin answered before Ernestine could say a word. "I believe you have business dealings with my father, Lord Fairfax?"

"Ah, yes, Your Excellency."

They entered a spacious, elegantly-furnished office. A dark old-looking desk stood against the window with two comfortable chairs in front of it.

"Please have a seat. My son will be here presently to read the Last Will and Testament of Mr. Fisher."

The young, or not so young, Mr. Gould entered, greeted them both warmly and started to read the testament. It was exactly as Mr. Fisher had told her. She inherited the gallery, a country house in the Cotswolds with all its contents, and two million pounds in cash, deposited at Barclays Bank. Ernestine was speechless. She had known about the gallery but did not know that Mr. Fisher owned a house in the country much less about that much cash. She looked at Robin who was still holding her hand.

"Please sign these documents," the older Mr. Gould said. Ernestine obliged; and when she was done, he shook her hand and said:

"Congratulations, Mrs. Leclerc, it was a pleasure doing business with you and should you have need of our services again, we are here to serve you. With these words the two solicitors left the room and Ernestine and Robin were shown out.

"This was short and to the point," Robin smiled, "and you got yourself quite a deal here, my old girl."

"I had no idea. Mr. Fisher only told me about the gallery and that made somewhat sense to me because I like the paintings he has."

"Let's go celebrate. I know this small restaurant not too far from here where we can get some decent food."

"I know you and little restaurants with decent food. They are usually high class establishments with excellent food creations."

Robin grinned and took her arm. They walked a short distance and entered another old building. On the second floor, a small bronze plate announced a restaurant. They entered and Ernestine saw someone waving at a table by the window. It was Lord Fairfax. They walked over there and Ernestine was pleased to see the old gentleman again.

"How are you dear Ernestine?" he inquired.

"I am well, thank you; and how are you keeping?"

"As well as can be expected, now that my workload is greatly reduced thanks to my son," and he proudly patted Robin on the shoulder.

They sat down and Ernestine noticed that a fourth set of cutlery was set and before she could think, Anette strolled to the table.

"Hey everyone, I hear that all went well with the Gould's?"

"Yes," Ernestine replied. "This part is done. Now I have to figure out what to do with the gallery and the country house."

"May I make some suggestions?" Lord Fairfax asked.

"Gladly," said Ernestine.

"You know that Anette here has been in charge of a Gallery in Boston for some years and it seems to me that she would be perfect to run the gallery here for you. As to the country house, let Robin look into it. Let's find out if it is in good repair and we can take it from there. As for the cash, you can figure that one out on your own."

Ernestine looked from one to the other. Suddenly, it dawned on her that they must have discussed the matter beforehand amongst themselves. She could not find fault with the plan and said:

"Could you run the gallery for me Anette? Would you even want to do this? It would require that you spend a lot of time in London and away from your parents. And you, Robin, would you come with me to the country house and take inventory? Or even better, could we all go?"

"I can only speak for myself. I would love to come and see the house of Mr. Fisher. I did not even know he owned one," replied Lord Fairfax with a twinkle in his old eyes.

And Robin said, "Of course I'll come with you Ernestine. I will make time for that."

"And you Anette? What do you say" asked Ernestine.

Anette got up and came around the table. She took Ernestine's hand and said, "I would love to run the gallery for you. I have missed the paintings and the art since I have left Boston. It was a dream I had of running a gallery in London, but that is all it was, a dream, until this moment when all of a sudden you make it possible." Tears ran down her cheeks and Robin got up and gently helped her back to her seat.

They ordered dinner and a fine bottle of wine and discussed their trip to the country house. It was decided to start early on Monday morning, look over the house, and be back in the city by nightfall.

Ernestine spent the weekend sorting out her belongings in the flat. In one room she put things to be picked up by the Salvation Army, in another the things she wanted to ship back to San Diego. There were also some handsome antiques that she and Robin had picked up on their excursions into the countryside. She decided to give some to Robin and Anette. She had a feeling that these two would not wait too long to announce their love to the world.

Late Sunday afternoon, the doorbell rang and Anette and Robin stood there with their hands full of little food bags. Ernestine had to laugh:

"You must have heard my belly rumbling. I haven't eaten all day and am starving."

"We picked up some Chinese food on the way over," said Anette. "We do not need plates, and the chopsticks are included also."

Robin looked around the place and stated:

"You really meant it when you said you were going to sort out your things."

"I have already arranged for the Salvation Army to come Tuesday morning to pick up some stuff. Some I will ship back to the States; and some are for you, provided you want them. Come and see!"

She showed them the few choice items she had marked for them. There was a bronze candelabra from the 18th century, some engraved silver serving plates in different sizes, and a set of beautifully-crafted hand-blown crystal glasses from Murano.

"These glasses are exquisite!" exclaimed Anette. "They will look just perfect in our living room cabinet. Don't you think so Robin?"

Robin just stared at her and then it dawned on Anette what she had just said. She blushed deeply and averted her eyes. Ernestine walked over to her and smilingly said:

"Congratulations you two. I had a feeling that there was more to it than just a casual friendship. I am so happy for you and wish you all the best always."

"You know, you are the first one to know," said Robin, sincerely.

"Oh, come on, your dad knows all about it," chuckled Ernestine.

"What do you mean?"

"I watched him watching you and I saw the contentment in his eyes. I know that he approves wholeheartedly and he will be pleased when you announce your union publicly. I think he would love to be able to attend the wedding of his only son."

"We will tell him tomorrow at the country house," Robin said and Anette agreed.

The three then sat down on whatever chair or pillow there was and devoured the delicious food. They talked until late, when the couple left, and Ernestine remained alone in the flat. She felt at peace and content. Somehow, all the pieces seem to fall into place and she would be able to hurry back to Eric very soon. The thought of him brought a frown to her face but faded quickly.

"I will tackle Eric when I get back and somehow it will also sort itself out. Life has a way of getting the best of me when I am not looking," thought Ernestine. She went to her bedroom, slipped under the covers and fell asleep immediately.

Chapter 29
The Country House

Early the next morning, the four left for Mr. Fisher's country house in Chipping Campden. They were amazed when they stopped in front of the house. It was a typical English Cottage with a low stone wall separating the sidewalk from the property and heart-shaped pavers leading to the wooden front door.

Three chimneys graced the thatched roof that gave the impression the house was wearing an old baseball cap. Most of the front wall was covered with still lush ivy. The cottage garden that meandered around the house was cleaned of dead flowers and awaited winter's sleep. Ernestine took the key out of her purse and opened the door.

They entered into a room that must have been used as a living room. Comfortable chairs were arranged around a huge fireplace, the low-hanging ceiling gave the room an air of coziness, and the dark wooden floorboards added to the charming atmosphere of the place. They walked silently through the house and tried to imagine Mr. Fisher staying here. Lord Fairfax was the first to break the silence:

"This seems to be the house of somebody quite different from the Mr. Fisher that I have known from the gallery," he said "he seemed to be almost timid and uneasy in his skin, whereas this house speaks of a man who enjoyed his life and was content with his circumstances."

The three friends nodded in agreement and Ernestine thought that it was interesting how we judge people by what they have and do, their looks and behaviors, without even knowing or caring what the person is actually like. Mr. Fisher was certainly a contradiction in more than one way; timorous and insecure at the gallery and a man of the world here in his country cottage.

Ernestine felt a pang of remorse because she also had very much misjudged her employer. She said a silent prayer for the rest of his soul and followed the others to the kitchen. It was a complete surprise. It was a chef's dream with the most sophisticated appliances, lots of counter space, a cook top with a griddle and a powerful, gleaming hood above it. The back splash was tiled with white marble, the same as the countertops.

The cupboards were filled with all things needed in a professional kitchen. A small bistro table with four chairs was set by one of the windows overlooking the herb garden. It was a bright and friendly kitchen that invited one to stay for a while. The four visitors were speechless and looked at one another uncomprehendingly.

"Why did he never say anything about this place?" wondered Lord Fairfax out loud and Ernestine nodded. She had her own ideas about why Mr. Fisher had kept this place a secret. She figured that he needed a place where he could be himself, had the privacy he needed, and to regain a clear head to deal with his customers at the gallery. She turned and proceeded to double doors that stood ajar.

She entered and found herself in a beautifully-appointed bedroom. Large windows were framed by heavy velvet curtains in a green hue matching the lampshades standing on the nightstands. One of Constable's early pictures hung over the bed.

When Lord Fairfax entered and saw the priceless painting, a muffled cry escaped his throat. Mr. Fisher had perfectly matched the green of "The Cornfield" with the curtains and lampshades. It seemed that the room was an extension of the painting and that one had entered a different time altogether.

Robin, who was not affected by the painting, broke the silence and said:

"We have to inventory this house carefully. Who knows what treasures it may hold. I can have a reputable firm come out here and do this for you, Ernestine. Just say the word."

"Oh, please do. I do not know where to start and my time here is rather limited," she answered.

"Then it is settled. I will arrange it and then send you the inventory report. That will give you also time to decide what you want to do with this house."

They stepped out into the back yard where an untamed small brook ran over moss-covered stones, eager to reach a point beyond the far hills. Three majestic willows gave shade to a sitting area delicately positioned beneath the canopy of these ancient trees whose history stretches back to Roman times. Ernestine followed the creek to the living fence and a strange stillness descended upon her.

Something caught her eye and she reached into the cold water to retrieve the glittering thing. It was a small ring with an unusual dark blue stone and an inscription that she could not decipher. She showed it to Lord Fairfax who took it from her hand, held it against the sun, and said:

"The inscription says: Love Forever." He gave the ring back to Ernestine and returned to the house. Slowly, Ernestine followed him and asked:

"You know this ring, don't you?"

"Yes, I gave it to the love of my life, Robin's mother. The color of the stone matched her eyes."

He turned his back on Ernestine and looked out of the window, lost in thought. Quietly, Ernestine went outside and called the others that it was time to go home. She did not mention the ring, but kept it in her purse.

The trip back was uneventful and nobody was in a talkative mood. They dropped Ernestine off at her flat and Robin and Anette would pick her up the next day to discuss the arrangements to be made regarding the gallery. They separated and Ernestine thoughtfully ascended the stairs to her flat.

"What a day," she thought. "Plenty to think about."

The next few days passed very quickly. The arrangements for the gallery were handed over to the solicitors at Gould's who would send her the finished contract for her review to San Diego. The Salvation Army had picked up the donations; the boxes had been shipped; and Robin and Anette had taken their gifts.

The flat was empty and ready to be returned to the rental agency. Ernestine took one last look around the flat where she had stayed for almost a year and was sad that another chapter of her life was closing. She was staying one last night at the Mayfair Hotel, before she returned to California.

Robin and Anette had invited her to dinner but she had gracefully declined. She needed to spend this evening by herself, in this city that had given her so much and that would always be a part of her. She had thought of contacting Sam one last time but then decided against it. It was better to keep him as a beautiful memory, tucked away in the recesses of her mind.

Chapter 30
One More Trip

The plane landed on time at San Diego's Lindbergh Field and Ernestine collected her belongings and headed for the exit. Her luggage was already on the carrousel and Mr. Connor was waiting for her. It was dark outside and light rain was falling. The streets shimmered as if diamonds had been strewn about by invisible hands. Ernestine shivered in her coat and quickly followed Mr. Connor to the waiting car.

He dropped her off at her apartment and she hurried into the warm lobby. The elevator rapidly brought her to her floor. She stepped into the hallway as the door to her apartment opened slowly. Astonished, but too tired to worry, she entered the dimly-lit foyer and stared at the wheelchair in the middle of the room. Eric held out his hands and Ernestine took two quick steps toward him and held him close to her.

From the corner of her eye she saw a movement by the kitchen and looked up. It was Emilia, a smile all over her friendly face.

"Welcome home, Ernestine," she said.

Ernestine got to her feet and hugged the older woman, with tears in her eyes.

"What does this mean? Eric, are you ready to go home?"

"Yes," he answered happily," we can go home whenever you like. Emilia was kind enough to take me here and drop me into your lap. She figured it would please you. Does it, Ernestine?" he asked sheepishly.

"This is the best news I could have wished for. Let's have a party. I'll order some food and you, Emilia, you must stay."

Happy, Ernestine turned around when the lights in the living room came slowly on and she stared at people that looked faintly familiar to her. Then it hit her, it was the staff from the hospital. Most of Eric's caretakers were there to celebrate with him his release into a new life. There was take-out pizza from the little Italian restaurant around the corner, Mexican finger foods, and plenty of sweets. It was a wonderful homecoming for both Ernestine and Eric. Gradually, people started to leave and Emilia took Ernestine aside.

"Eric has recovered to a point that astonished our most pessimistic doctors. He will do well in your care. Eventually, we all hope he will be able to leave the wheelchair behind and walk on his own two feet. We have made arrangements for him to see our best Physiotherapist twice a week at the hospital. But if you want to leave Southern California, just let us know and we'll find someone for him wherever you two may go."

"I don't know what to say," whispered Ernestine. "You have all been such caring people; thank you so much for everything."

Emilia gave her a big hug, turned to Eric and gave him a big hug, and then quickly left the apartment.

Finally, they were alone, staring at each other. Eric broke the silence and said, "You look awfully tired; go to bed and we'll talk tomorrow."

"Okay," a worn-out Ernestine replied. "We'll talk tomorrow." She kissed him on the cheek and went to bed, too tired to figure all this out.

The sun was shining brightly when Ernestine opened her eyes and the smell of freshly-brewed coffee wafted through the apartment. She put on her housecoat and followed her nose to the kitchen. Eric had made fresh coffee and was preparing breakfast. Ernestine stood still and watched him for a while. He was able to move around quite easily in the wheelchair. He opened the fridge and tried to reach the eggs on the top shelf. After a few fruitless attempts he slumped back into the chair. Ernestine felt a sharp pain seeing him like this and said gaily, "It smells heavenly here and I would love to have a cup of coffee."

Eric turned around and somberly stared at her.

"Have you been standing there long?" he wanted to know.

"Long enough to realize that the eggs are out of your reach and that you need me," Ernestine replied with a broad smile on her face. She went over to the fridge and handed the eggs to Eric who silently put them on the counter.

"Let's get something straight right from the beginning," Ernestine said, "as long as you need the wheelchair I will help you but only if you ask. You are almost as good as new and the prognosis is excellent for you to be back to your usual self in a short time. Until then, promise me, you will not let the wheelchair darken your mood."

Astonished, Eric looked at Ernestine:

"What are you saying?"

"That after Thanksgiving, you and I and the wheelchair are going back to Oregon to your charming house by the small lake. I want to spend this Christmas there with you. After that, we will see what is going to happen. But now, let's make some ham and eggs. I am hungry."

With these words, she took the ham out of the fridge and Eric started to make toast. Soon breakfast was ready and they enjoyed the home-cooked meal.

Soon thereafter, the hospital van picked up Eric, and Ernestine promised to drive up to the hospital in the afternoon. She quickly showered and went to the downtown grocery store to buy the turkey and all the trimmings. Having stowed everything in her fridge, she drove to the hospital where she first went to see Emilia.

They discussed the best course to take with Eric and Ernestine promised to keep her up-to-date with the progress he would be making. It was decided that a couple of weeks after Thanksgiving they could go back to Oregon. Emilia hoped that by then Eric would no longer need the wheelchair but kept this to herself. She did not wish to give Ernestine false hope.

Both women walked down the long hallway to Eric's room and were surprised to see him sitting in a chair by the window reading. They sat down close to him and discussed the trip to Oregon. Emilia suggested renting a van to make it easy with the wheelchair and both Ernestine and Eric agreed. They were to leave within two weeks.

"I just bought a turkey and hope that you will join us, please Emilia?" said Ernestine.

"I will," she replied and got up. "See you around four in the afternoon on Thursday."

After she had closed the door, Ernestine and Eric made plans for their trip to Oregon.

Thanksgiving came and went and the day arrived when Eric had to leave the hospital that had been his home for the past months for good. The staff was there and bid him farewell. His main caregiver helped him out of the wheelchair and into the front seat and said:

"Now Eric, don't get any ideas. Let the lady drive. Driving yourself will have to wait a little longer. Remember, little steps are enough for you." He shook Eric's hands and gave him a bear hug.

Finally, everything was put in the van and Ernestine drove away. They took the same road that they had taken a few years back when Eric had picked up Ernestine from the same hospital. For a long time they were silent, each lost in memory of times past. They stayed at a little inn along the way and Eric managed quite well without his wheelchair.

Early next morning they drove on, and by nightfall they arrived at the house. The light was on and the caretaker was waiting for them. Ernestine had called ahead with the approximate arrival time and it was arranged that he would fill the fridge with the necessary items and be there when they arrived. He helped Eric up the stairs and put the luggage in the bedrooms. Ernestine thanked him and they decided that he would come around in the morning again.

"It feels good to be home again," said Eric seriously, but a smile played around the edges of his mouth. He stretched out his arms for Ernestine and she went to him. They kissed each other for the first time, gently at first but then more demandingly. They caressed each other and Eric sighed:

"I wish I could, but it will have to wait a little longer. Will you wait with me Ernestine?" he said with pleading eyes.

"Yes," she simply replied and put her head on his shoulder.

They remained on the sofa until the day turned into night.

Chapter 31
Home At Last

The morning came quickly and it took Ernestine a moment to realize where she was. A smile passed over her face when she recalled the past few days. She crawled out of the warm bed and walked toward the window, looking out at the sky where a string of broken clouds allowed teasing glimpses of sunshine painting the lake in subdued colors.

She donned a soft pink bathrobe and matching slippers, a gift from Robin, and softly opened the door to the hallway. Eric's door was ajar and she heard music playing inside. She pushed the door open and saw Eric sitting in his favorite chair by the window. He turned his head and waved to her.

"Good morning, Ernestine; did you sleep well?"

"I did," replied Ernestine, "and you?"

"Very well indeed, thank you. There is nothing like sleeping in one's own bed."

His eyes shone with pleasure and love, and Ernestine felt a warmth flowing through her that she recognized as the feeling of love, contentment, and happiness. She went to him and pulled a chair to the window. They both sat there for a moment, silent and deep in thought. At the same time, they started speaking and this little fact broke the awkwardness and they laughed and held hands.

"Let's go for a drive around town and the countryside after breakfast," said Ernestine, "provided you feel like it."

"Sounds like a good idea. We can also stop at the store. I need a few things," replied Eric.

So, it was decided and after breakfast they went to the car and drove off.

"How different the village now looks," thought Ernestine. "The last time I was here was after Jonathan's death and the world was empty and gray."

A strange feeling spread through Ernestine. It was no longer the painful feeling of Jonathan's death but gratitude that she had known him, and spent beautiful years with him. This emotion was so new to her that she had to stop at the side of the road and absorb it. Eric looked at her but did not break the silence. Somehow, he knew that there was a change going on within Ernestine that he should not interrupt. After a few minutes, Ernestine turned toward him and said, "Now I know that everything will be alright."

She did not elaborate but started the car and they headed back to the cabin. There was a car parked in the driveway and Ernestine wondered who the visitor could be. She opened her door and almost fell over when a black furry bundle jumped up on her.

"Tuesday!" she exclaimed, "How wonderful to see you again." The dog licked her hand and stayed close to her. Ernestine questioningly looked at Eric. "How..., is she going to stay with us?"

"Yes," he replied and Ernestine ran around the car and hugged him with tears in her eyes.

"Thank you so much. I don't know what to say; but it makes my day complete."

Ernestine and Tuesday disappeared in the house and Eric stayed outside talking to the caretaker. After a few minutes he followed them inside and saw both of them rolling on the floor. Ernestine reminded him of a young girl. He was glad he had asked the caretaker to bring Tuesday back. He knew how attached Ernestine was to her.

"Let me make something to eat for us after I feed Tuesday." And Ernestine busied herself in the kitchen. Within a short time she called out for Eric to join them. She had made a vegetable soup with the fresh bread they had bought in the village. They silently ate their meal, watching Tuesday devouring hers.

After dinner they went outside and sat down on the soft outdoor sofa. They were quiet for quite some time, each one deep in thought. Silently, they watched the deep blue sky turning a dark indigo while the first stars shyly appeared. After a while, the whole sky was full of shimmering stars reminding Ernestine of a royal cloak she once saw at the Tower of London when she spent a summer as a child with her beloved grandmother. The stars looked like tiny jewels sewn onto a satin cloth.

The lake was dark and forbidding and once in a while tiny ripples broke the mirror-like surface. The trees stood guard over all of them with their proud heads held high into the night sky. The night wind softly whispered its eternal song and the trees nodded their agreement with the words only nature understands.

"This is beautiful; the stars, the sky, the whole world," she whispered to no one in particular.

Gently, ever so gently, Eric took her face into his hands and held it tenderly. He kissed her on her waiting lips, slowly, thoughtfully. When her lips parted, his tongue traced the soft fullness of her lips. For Ernestine the touch of his lips was a delicious sensation and she was awash with feelings she had not had in a very long time.

His lips were sweet and warm on hers and she wished it would always be like this. She shivered under his caresses and slowly met his gaze. She put her arms around him and pulled him closer. An aching need for another kiss flooded her whole body and she covered his mouth with slow, trembling kisses.

"Will you stay with me and be my friend and wife?" Eric asked in a hushed voice.

Ernestine simply said … "Yes."

They both turned their gaze again toward the night sky and took a solemn vow to always be here for one another and nothing in this world would ever come between them. A shooting star crossed the sky and both Ernestine and Eric understood that their union was meant to be.

The End